A Night In The LONESOME OCTOBER

ROGER ZELAZNY

Illustrations by
GAHAN WILSON

An AvoNova Book

William Morrow and Company, Inc.

New York

AVON BOOKS
A division of
The Hearst Corporation
1350 Avenue of the Americas
New York, New York 10019

Text copyright © 1993 by The Amber Corporation
Illustrations copyright © 1993 by Gahan Wilson
Published by arrangement with the author
Library of Congress Catalog Card Number: 93-18414
ISBN: 0-688-12508-5

Library of Congress Cataloging in Publication Data:
Zelazny, Roger.
    A night in the lonesome October / Roger Zelazny.
        p.   cm.
I. Title.
PS3576.E43N5   1993   93-18414
813'.54—dc20   CIP

First Morrow/AvoNova Printing: August 1993

AVONOVA TRADEMARK REG. U.S. PAT. OFF. AND IN OTHER COUNTRIES, MARCA REGISTRADA, HECHO EN U.S.A.

Printed in the U.S.A.

ARC   10   9   8   7   6   5   4   3   2   1

To—*Mary Shelley*
Edgar Allan Poe
Bram Stoker
Sir Arthur Conan Doyle
H.P. Lovecraft
Ray Bradbury
Robert Bloch
Albert Payson Terhune
and the makers of
a lot of old movies—

Thanks.

Contents

CONTENTS

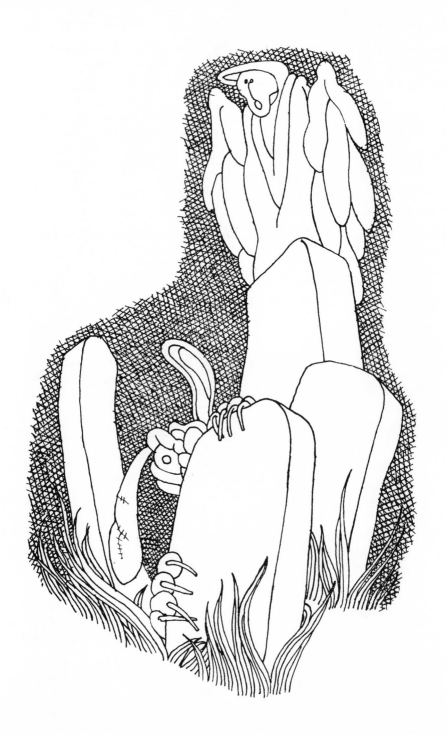

A Night in the Lonesome October

I AM A WATCHDOG. MY NAME IS SNUFF. I LIVE with my master Jack outside of London now. I like Soho very much at night with its smelly fogs and dark streets. It is silent then and we go for long walks. Jack is under a curse from long ago and must do much of his work at night to keep worse things from happening. I keep watch while he is about it. If someone comes, I howl.

We are the keepers of several curses and our work is very important. I have to keep watch on the Thing in the Circle, the Thing in the Wardrobe, and the Thing in the Steamer Trunk—not to mention the Things in the Mirror. When they try to get out I raise particular hell with them. They are afraid of me. I do not know what I would do if they all tried to get out at the same time. It is good exercise, though, and I snarl a lot.

I fetch things for Jack on occasion—his wand, his

big knife with the old writing on the sides. I always know just when he needs them because it is my job to watch and to know. I like being a watchdog better than what I was before he summoned me and gave me this job.

So we walk, Jack and I, and other dogs are often afraid of me. Sometimes I like to talk and compare notes on watchdogging and masters, but I do tend to intimidate them.

One night when we were in a graveyard recently an old watchdog came by, though, and we talked for a time.

"Hi. I'm a watchdog."

"Me, too."

"I've been watching you."

"And I've been watching you."

"Why is your person digging a big hole?"

"There are some things down there that he needs."

"Oh. I don't think he's supposed to be doing that."

"May I see your teeth?"

"Yes. Here. May I see yours?"

"Of course."

"Perhaps it's all right. Do you think you might leave a large bone somewhere nearby?"

"I believe that could be arranged."

"Are you the ones who were by here last month?"

"No, that was the competition. We were shopping elsewhere."

"They didn't have a watchdog."

"Bad planning. What did you do?"

"Barked a lot. They got nervous and left."

"Good. Then we're still probably ahead."

"Been with your person long?"

"Ages. How long've you been a graveyard dog?"

"All my life."

"Like it?"

"It's a living," he said.

Jack needed lots of ingredients for his work, as there was a big bit of business due soon. Perhaps it were best to take it day by day.

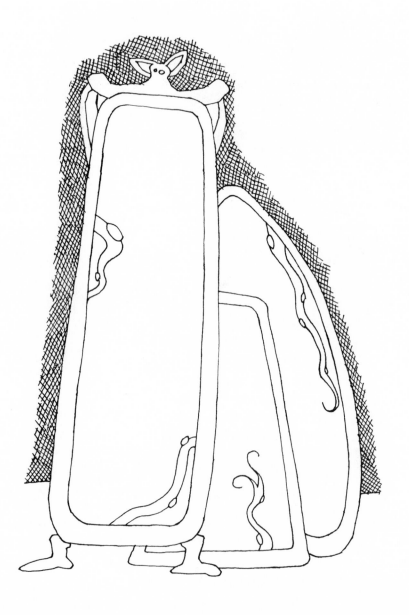

October 1

ADE THE CIRCUITS. THE THING IN THE
Circle changed shapes, finally making itself look like a
lady dog of attractive person and very friendly disposition. But I was not fooled into breaking the
Circle. It didn't have the smell part down yet.

"Nice try," I told it.

"You'll get yours, mutt," it said.

I walked past the various mirrors. The Things locked
in them gibbered and writhed. I showed them my teeth
and they writhed away.

The Thing in the Steamer Trunk pounded on the
sides and hissed and sputtered when it became aware
of my sniffing about. I snarled. It hissed again. I
growled. It shut up.

I made my way to the attic then and checked out
the Thing in the Wardrobe. It was scratching on the
sides when I entered but grew still as I approached.

"How's everything inside?" I asked.

"Be a lot better if someone could be persuaded to turn the key with his paws."

"Better for you maybe."

"I could find you lots of great bones—big ones, fresh, juicy, lots of meat on them."

"I just ate, thanks."

"What *do* you want?"

"Nothing special just now."

"Well, I want out. Figure what it's worth to you and let's talk."

"You'll get your chance, by and by."

"I don't like waiting."

"Tough."

"Up yours, hound."

"Tsk, tsk," I replied, and I went away when it began using more abusive language.

I went back downstairs, then passed through the library, smelling its musty volumes and incense, spices, herbs, and other interesting matters, on my way to the parlor, whence I stared out the window at the day. Watching, of course. That is my job.

October 2

WE TOOK A WALK LAST NIGHT, ACQUIRING mandrake root in a field far from here at the place of a killing by somebody else. The master wrapped it in silk and took it to his work space direct. I could hear him engage in good-natured banter with the Thing in the Circle. Jack has a long list of ingredients, and things must be done properly on schedule.

The cat Graymalk came slinking about, pussyfoot, peering in our windows. Ordinarily, I have little against cats. I can take them or leave them, I mean. But Graymalk belongs to Crazy Jill who lives over the hill, in towards town, and Graymalk was spying for her mistress, of course. I growled to let her know she had been spotted.

"About your watching early, faithful Snuff," she hissed.

"About your spying early," I responded, "Gray."

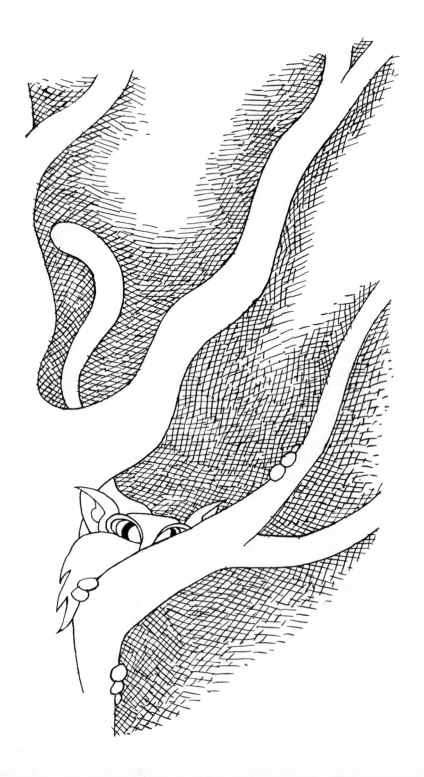

"We have our tasks."

"We do."

"And so it has begun."

"It has."

"Goes it well?"

"So far. And you?"

"The same. I suppose it is easiest simply to ask this way, for now."

". . . But cats are sneaky," I added.

She tossed her head, raised a paw and studied it.

"There are certain pleasures to be had in lurking."

"For cats," I said.

". . . And certain knowledges gained."

"Such as . . . ?"

"I am not the first come calling here today. My predecessor left traces. Are you aware of this, faithful watcher?"

"No," I replied. "Who was it?"

"The owl, Nightwind, consort of Morris and MacCab. I saw him flee at dawn, found a feather out back. The feather is tainted with mummy dust, to do you ill."

"Why do you tell me this?"

"Perhaps because I am a cat and it amuses me to be arbitrary and do you a good turn. I shall take the feather away with me and leave it at their window, concealed amid shrubs."

"I prowled last night after my walk," I said. "I was near your house beyond the hill. I saw Quicklime, the black snake who lives in the belly of the mad monk, Rastov. He rubbed against your doorpost, shedding scales."

"Ah! And why do you tell me this?"

"I pay my debts."

"There should not be debts between our folk."

"This is between us."

"You are a strange hound, Snuff."

"You are a strange cat, Graymalk."

"As it should be, I daresay."

And she was gone amid shadows. As it should be.

October 3

WE WALKED AGAIN LAST NIGHT, AND THE master was hunting. He had donned his cloak and said to me, "Snuff, fetch!" And from the way he said it, I knew that it was the blade he required. I took it to him and we went out. Our luck was varied. That is, he obtained the ingredients he was after, but only with considerable turmoil and an inordinate passage of time. We were discovered near the end. I gave warning, and we had to flee. It was a long chase, till finally I hung back and nipped the other on the leg. We made good our escape, with the ingredients. As he was washing up later, Jack told me I was an excellent watchdog. I was very proud.

Later, he let me out to prowl. I checked Rastov's place, which was dark. Out and about business, I supposed. Lying behind a bush near Crazy Jill's, I could hear her chuckling within and talking to Graymalk.

They had already been out. The broom beside the rear entrance was still warm.

I was especially careful at Morris and MacCab's. Nightwind can be very potent after dark and could be anywhere.

I heard a small tittering from the nearly bare branches of a cherry tree. I sniffed the air, but Nightwind's gritty signature was not on it. There was something else, though.

The small laughter—so high-pitched a human might not hear it—came again.

"Who's there?" I asked.

A cluster of leaves unrolled itself from the tree and darted down, stitching the air at blinding speeds about my head.

"Another who watches," came its tiny voice.

"The neighborhood is getting crowded," I said. "You may call me Snuff. What may I call you?"

"Needle," it replied. "Whom do you serve?"

"Jack," I answered. "And yourself?"

"The Count," it said.

"Do you know whether Morris and MacCab found their ingredients?"

"Yes," it replied. "Do you know whether the crazy woman found hers?"

"I'm pretty sure she did."

"So she is abreast of us. Still, it is early. . . ."

"When did the Count join the Game?"

"Two nights ago," it said.

"How many players are there?"

"I don't know," it answered. Then it soared high and was gone.

Life was suddenly even more complicated, and I'd no way of knowing whether they were openers or closers.

As I made my way back I felt that I was being watched. But whoever it was, was very, very good. I could not spot him, so I took a long, long way about. He left me later to follow another. I hurried home to report.

October 4

RAINY DAY. WINDY, TOO. I MADE MY ROUNDS.
"Up yours, cur."
"Same to you."
"Hi, things."
Slither, slither.
"How's about letting me out?"
"Nope."
"My day will come."
"It's not today."
The usual. Everything seemed in order.
"How's about a collie? You like redheads?"
"You still haven't got it right. S'long."
"Son of a bitch!"
I checked all the windows and doors from the
inside, then let myself out the back through my pri-
vate hatch, master Jack sleeping or resting in his
darkened room. I checked everything again from the
outside. I could discover no surprises of the sort I had

discussed with Graymalk the other day. But I did find something else: There was a single paw-print, larger than my own, in the shelter of a tree to the side of the house. The accompanying scent and any adjacent prints had been washed away by the rain. I circled far afield, seeking more evidence of the intruder, but there was nothing else. The old man who lives up the road was in his yard, harvesting mistletoe from a tree, using a small, shining sickle. A squirrel sat upon his shoulder. This was a new development.

I addressed the squirrel through a hedge:

"Are you in the Game?"

It scurried to the man's nearer shoulder and peered.

"Who asks?" it chattered.

"Call me Snuff," I answered.

"Call me Cheeter," it replied. "Yes, I suppose we are. Last minute thing—rush, rush."

"Opener or closer?"

"Impolite! Impolite to ask! You know that!"

"Just thought I'd try. You could be novices."

"Not new enough to be giving anything away. Leave it at that."

"I will."

"Stay. Is there a black snake in it?"

"You ask me to give something away. But yes, there is: Quicklime. Beware. His master is mad."

"Aren't they all?"

We chuckled and I faded away.

That evening we went out again. We crossed the bridge and walked for a long, long while. The dour detective and his rotund companion were about, the latter limping from his adventure of the other night. We passed them twice in the fog. But it was the wand

Jack bore this night, to stand at the city's center with it and trap a certain beam of starlight in a crystal vial while the clocks chimed twelve. Immediately, the liquid in the container began to glow with a reddish light; and somewhere in the distance a howling rose up. No one I knew. I wasn't even sure it was a dog. It said a single word in the language of my kind, a long, drawn-out "Lost!" My hackles rose at the sound of it.

"Why are you growling, friend?" Jack asked.

I shook my head. I was not sure.

October 5

I BREAKFASTED IN THE DARK AND MADE MY rounds of the house. Everything was in good order. The master was asleep so I let myself out and prowled the vicinity. The day would not begin for some time yet.

I walked beyond the hill, to Crazy Jill's place. The house was dark and quiet. Then I turned to head for Rastov's ramshackle abode. I caught a scent as I did, and I sought its source. A small form lay unmoving atop the garden wall.

"Graymalk," I said. "Sleeping?"

"Never wholly," came the reply. "Catnappery is useful. What are you after, Snuff?"

"Checking an idea I had. It doesn't really involve you or your lady—directly. I'll be walking to Rastov's place now."

Suddenly, she was gone from the wall. A moment later she was near. I glimpsed a glint of yellow light from her eyes.

"I'll walk with you, if it's not secret work."

"Come, then."

We walked, and after a time I asked, "Everything quiet?"

"At our place, yes," she replied. "But I heard there was a killing in town earlier. Your work?"

"No. We were in town, but it was a different sort of work we were about. Where did you hear of it?"

"Nightwind was by. We talked a little. He'd been across the river into town. A man was torn apart, as by a particularly vicious dog. I thought of you."

"Not me, not me," I said.

"There must be more of these, of course, as the others seek their ingredients. This will make the people wary, the streets better patrolled between now and the big event."

"I suppose so. Pity."

We reached Rastov's place. A small light burned within.

"He works late."

"Or very early."

"Yes."

In my mind, I traced a path back to my own home. Then I turned and headed across fields to the old farmhouse where Morris and MacCab resided. Graymalk continued with me. A piece of the moon began to rise. Clouds slid quickly across the sky, their bellies tickled by the light. Graymalk's eyes flashed.

When we reached the place I stood among long grasses. There were lights within.

"More work," she said.

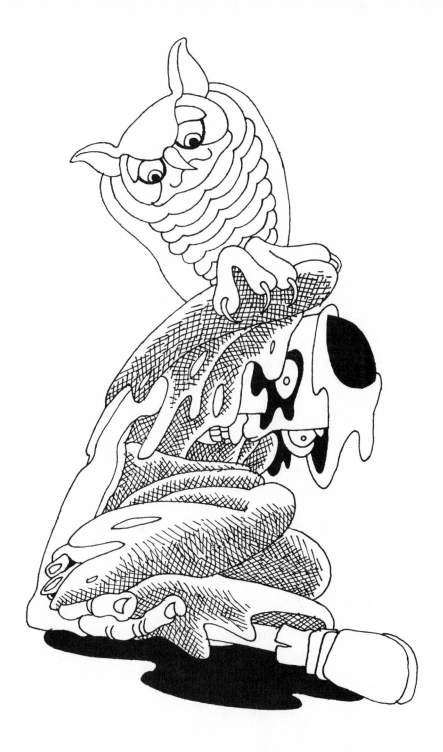

"Who?" came Nightwind's voice from atop the barn.

"Shall we answer?"

"Why not?" I said.

She offered her name. I growled my own. Nightwind departed his perch to circle us, finally alighting nearby.

"You know each other," he remarked.

"We are acquainted."

"What do you want here?"

"I wanted to ask you about that killing in town," I said. "You saw it?"

"Only after it had occurred and been discovered."

"So you did not see which of us was about it?"

"No. If indeed it were one of us."

"How many of us are there, Nightwind? Can you tell me that?"

"I don't know that such knowledge should be dispensed. It may come under my prohibitions."

"A trade then? We list the ones we know. If there is one among them you do not know, you furnish us with another we do not know—if you can."

He swiveled his head around backwards to think, then said, "That sounds fair. It would save us all time. Very well. You know of my masters, and I know both of yours. That's four."

"Then there is Rastov, with Quicklime," Graymalk offered. "Five."

"I know of them," he responded.

"The old man who lives up the road from me seems of druidical persuasion," I said. "I saw him harvesting mistletoe the old way, and he has a friend—a squirrel called Cheeter."

"Oh?" Nightwind remarked. "I was unaware of this."

"The man's name is Owen," Graymalk stated. "I've been watching them. And that's six."

Nightwind said, "For three nights now a small, hunched man has been raiding graveyards. I saw him on my patrols. Two nights back I followed him by the full of the moon. He bore his gleanings to a large farmhouse to the south of here—a place with many lightning rods, above which a perpetual storm rages. Then he delivered them to a tall, straight man he addressed as the 'Good Doctor.' It may be they are seven, or perhaps eight."

"Would you show us this place?" I asked.

"Follow me."

We did, and after a long trek we came to the farmhouse. There were lights in its basement but the windows were curtained and we could not see what the Good Doctor was about. There were many odors of death in the air, however.

"Thank you, Nightwind," I said. "Have you any others?"

"No. Have you?"

"No."

"Then I would say that we are even."

He took wing and hurried off through the night.

As I crouched sniffing near a window I traced trails from Morris and MacCab's place to this one, from this one to Crazy Jill's, to my own, to Owen's, from Owen's to the others'. . . . It was hard keeping all of the trails in mind at once.

I leaped at the bright flash and the crackling sound from behind the window. The smell of ozone reached me moments later, and the sound of wild laughter.

"Yes, this place will bear watching," Graymalk observed, from her sudden perch high in a nearby tree. "Shall we go now?"

"Yes."

We headed back and I left her at Jill's—dropping the adjective out of politeness in her presence—and I left her to catnappery on her wall. When I returned home I found another paw-print.

October 6

EXCITEMENT. I HEARD THE MIRROR CRACK this morning, and I ran and raised holy hell before it, keeping the slitherers inside. Jack heard the fuss and fetched his mundane wand and transferred them all to another mirror, just like the Yellow Emperor. This one was much smaller, which may teach them a lesson, but probably not. We're not sure how they did it. Continued pressure on some flaw, most likely. Good thing they're afraid of me.

Jack retired and I went outside. The sun was shining through gray and white clouds and only the crisp scents of autumn rode the breezes. I had been drawing lines in my head during the night. What I'd tried to do would have been much easier for Nightwind, Needle, or even Cheeter. It is hard for an earthbound creature to visualize the terrain in the manner I'd attempted. But I'd drawn lines from each of our houses to each of the others. The result was an elaborate diagram with an outer boundary and intersecting rays within. And once I have such a figure I can do things with it that the others cannot. It was necessarily incomplete because I did not know the whereabouts of the Count—or of any other players who might not yet have come to my attention.

Nevertheless, it was enough to play around with, was sufficient for seeking some approximation.

I began walking.

My way took me through yard and field to a lane which I followed for a time. When I reached what I deemed to be the proper spot I halted. There were several large old trees off to my left, another across the way to the right. The spot which I had so carefully derived by means of my mental mapmaking was situated, unfortunately, in the middle of the road. And it hadn't even the good grace to be a crossroad.

The nearest house was to my right and back several hundred yards along the way I had come. It was inhabited, I knew, by an elderly couple who fed birds, worked in their garden, and argued every Saturday night when the old man staggered in from the pub. In my earlier investigations of the area I had seen no signs that they might be involved in the Game.

I decided to sniff about, anyway. As I sought along the roadsides I heard a familiar voice:

"Snuff!"

"Nightwind! Where are you?"

"Overhead. There's a hollow place in this tree. Stayed out too long. Came in here to get away from the light. We think a bit alike, don't we?"

"Looks like we draw the same lines."

"This can't be the place, though."

"No. It's the center of the pattern we have, but it's not a likely spot."

"Therefore the pattern is incomplete. But we knew that. We don't know where the Count is."

"If he's the only other. It must take place at the center of the pattern we form."

"Yes. What should we do?"

"Could you follow Needle back to the Count's place?"

"Bats are damnably erratic."

"I couldn't do it. And I don't think Graymalk could."

"No. Never trust a cat, anyway. All they're good for is stringing tennis racquets."

"Will you *try* following Needle?"

"First I have to find the little bastard. But yes, I'll watch for him tonight."

"Let me know what you find?"

"I'll think about it."

"It might be to your advantage, if you ever need an errand run by day."

"That's true. All right. Why do the players always form themselves into a pattern around the center of things, anyway?"

"Beats me," I said.

I returned home, growling at the Things in the Mirror—propped in the front hallway now—as I passed, just to let them know I was on the job. The Thing in the Steamer Trunk was still. I told the Thing in the Wardrobe to shut up. Its pounding was shaking the place. I had to bark several times to get it to be quiet.

Down in the cellar the Thing in the Circle had become a Pekingese.

"You like little ladies?" it asked. "Come and get it, big fella."

It still smelled of Thing rather than dog.

"You're not really very bright," I said.

The Peke gave me the paw as I departed, and it's hard to turn your leg that way.

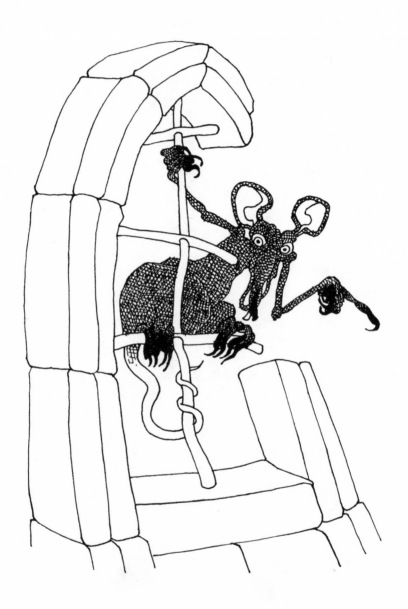

October 7

WE WERE OUT AGAIN LAST NIGHT IN PURSUIT of more ingredients for the Great Work. It was very foggy, and there were many patrolmen about. This did not stop us, but it made things more difficult. The master's blade flashed, the woman screamed, and there was a rending of garments. We passed the Great Detective in our flight, and I inadvertently tripped his companion, whose limp had lessened his ability to avoid onrushing canines.

As we crossed the bridge Jack unrolled the strip of cloth and regarded it.

"Very good. It *is* green," he remarked.

Why his list of materials required the edge of a green cloak worn by a red-haired lady on this date at midnight and removed while still upon her person, I am uncertain. Magical rotas sometimes strike me as instructions for lunatic scavenger hunts. Nonetheless, Jack was happy so I was, too.

Much later, after an unsuccessful search for Night-wind, I returned home and was drowsing in the parlor when I heard a small scratching sound from the rear of the house. It did not come again. So I went into my stalking mode and investigated.

The kitchen was empty, the pantry was bare. I circulated.

At the entrance to the front hall I caught the scent. I halted, watched, listened. I became aware of a slight movement—low, and to my right—ahead.

It sat before the mirror watching the slitherers. I suspended breathing and edged forward. When I was near enough to catch it with a short lunge I said, "I trust you are finding your last moments amus-ing."

It leaped and I was upon it, catching it at the base of the neck—a large, black rat.

"Wait! I can explain!" it said. "Snuff! You're Snuff! I came to see you!"

I waited, neither tightening nor loosening my hold. A toss of my head would snap its spine.

"Needle told me of you," it went on. "Cheeter told me where to find you."

I couldn't say anything, my mouth being occupied. So I continued to wait.

"Cheeter said you seemed reasonable, and I wanted to talk. Nobody was around outside, so I let myself in through the little door in the back. Could you put me down, please?"

I carried the rat to a corner, deposited him there, seating myself directly before him.

"So you are in the Game," I said.

"Yes."

"Then you must know that entering another player's home without invitation lays you open to immediate reprisal."

"Yes, but it was the only way I knew to get in touch with you."

"What is it you wanted to tell me?"

"I know Quicklime, and Quicklime knows Nightwind. . . ."

"Yes?"

"Quicklime says that Nightwind told him you know a lot about who the players are and what they're about. And that you sometimes trade information. I'd like to trade some."

"Why didn't you trade directly with Nightwind?"

"I've never met Nightwind. Owls scare me. Besides, I heard he's pretty closebeaked. Keeps everything close to his feathers, and keeps his pinions to himself."

He chuckled at that. I did not.

"If you just wanted to talk, why were you snooping around?" I asked.

"I couldn't help being curious when I saw the things in the mirror."

"Is this the first time you've been by?"

"Yes!"

"Who're you with?"

"The Good Doctor."

"I've a friend named Graymalk who happens to be a cat. She comes around here a lot. If I think you're planning to make mischief I'm going to let her start coming in regularly."

"I'm not looking for trouble, damn it! Let's keep the cat out of this!"

"Okay. What are you trading and what do you want?"

"I want you to tell me everybody you know who's in the Game, and where they live."

"What do I get?"

"I know where the Count takes his rest."

"Nightwind was going to seek that information."

"He's not good enough to follow Needle through the woods. Owls can't zigzag the way bats can."

"You may be right. You will take me to the place?"

"Yes. For a list of the others."

"All right," I said. "But you came to me. I get to make the terms. Show me the place first. Then I'll tell you who else is playing."

"I agree."

"And what may I call you?"

"Bubo," he replied.

I backed away.

"Let's go," I said.

Outside, it was chill, windy, and damp. A few clouds hung low in the west. The stars seemed very near.

"Which way?" I asked.

He indicated the southeast and headed in that direction. I followed.

He crossed several fields, coming at length to a stand of trees. He entered there.

"These are the woods where Needle might lose Nightwind?" I said.

"Yes."

He led me among trees. Finally, we came to a very rocky clearing, and he halted.

"Yes?" I said.

"This is the place."

"What is it?"

"The remains of an old church."

I walked forward, sniffing. Nothing untoward. . . .

I climbed the low hill on which the ruins stood. Among the blocks of stone I saw an opening. When I peered within I saw that it continued downward.

". . . Goes back," I said, "as if this wasn't always ground level. As if much of it were covered up, overgrown. . . . We're actually standing above the ruin, aren't we?"

"I don't know. I've never been down in it," he replied. "That isn't the spot. The cemetery's down the hill, over that way."

He headed in the direction he'd indicated, and I followed. There were a few fallen, half-buried markers about. Then there was a bigger place, I realized, when I saw that lines of stone in the ground were what had been the tops of walls of a crypt. Weeds grew amid them. Bubo rushed forward, stood in their midst.

"See, there's a hole here," he told me. "His stuff's down there."

I moved toward it, looked inside. It was too dark for me to distinguish anything. I wished Nightwind or Graymalk had been along.

"I'll have to take your word for it," I said, "for now."

"Then tell me the names and places you'd promised."

"I'll tell you as we walk along—away from here."

"Does this place make you nervous?"

"It's not a month for taking chances," I said.

He laughed.

"That's very funny," he said.

"It is, isn't it?" I replied.

The dying moon came up above the trees, lighting our way.

With midnight's chimes speech comes to me. I rose and stretched, waiting for them to cease. Jack, having roused himself especially for the occasion, watched me with a mixture of amusement and interest.

"Busy day, Snuff?" he asked.

"We'd a visitor while you napped. The rat Bubo," I said, "companion of the Good Doctor."

"And?"

"We traded. A list of the players for the location of the Count's grave. He said it was in the cemetery to a ruined church to the southeast. Showed me the place."

"Good work," Jack replied. "How does this affect your calculations?"

"Hard to say. I'm going to think about it, and then I'll need to do some walking."

"Still early in the Game," he said. "You know how the picture can change."

"True," I replied. "But at least we're somewhat better-informed than we were. Of course, we must check the content of the crypt by day, to be certain. I think I can persuade Graymalk to do that."

"Not Quicklime?"

"I trust the cat more. I'd rather share information with her, if it must be shared."

"You know her persuasion, then?"

I shook my head.

"No, I'm just going by my feelings."

"Has she spoken of her mistress, Jill?"

"Not in any detail."

"I believe the lady is younger than she causes herself to appear."

"That may be. I just don't know. I haven't met her."

"I have. Let me know if the cat talks party politics."

"I will, but she won't—not unless I do, and I'm not about to."

"You're the best judge of that situation."

"Yes. Neither of us has anything to gain by volunteering information at this time. But we might stand to lose something in the way of cooperation. Unless you've some overriding need for the information that I don't know about. In that case, though. . . ."

"I understand. No. Let it be. Have you learned it for any of the others?"

"No. Are we going out tonight?"

"No. We're set, for now. Have you any plans?"

"A little calculation and a lot of rest."

"Sounds like a good idea."

"Do you remember that time in Dijon, when that lady from the other side managed to distract you?"

"It's hard to forget. Why do you ask?"

"No special reason. Just reminiscing. Good night, Jack."

I moved to my favorite corner and settled with my head upon my paws.

" 'Night, Snuff."

I listened to his retreating footsteps. It was time to visit Growler, for a workshop in advanced stalking. Soon the world went away.

©ctober 8

I DREW MORE LINES IN MY HEAD LAST NIGHT and this morning, but before I'd created a satisfactory picture we had a caller.

I barked twice when the door chimes sounded, because it was expected of me. The master went to the door and I followed.

A tall, solidly built man, dark-haired, was on the stoop, and he smiled.

"Hello," he said, "my name's Larry Talbot. I'm your new neighbor, and I thought I'd come by and pay my respects."

"Won't you come in and have a cup of tea with me?" Jack said.

"Thank you."

Jack led him into the parlor and seated him, excused himself, and went to the kitchen. I stayed in the parlor and watched. Talbot glanced several times at the palm of his hand. Then he studied me.

"Good boy," he said.

I opened my mouth, let my tongue hang out, and panted a few times. But I did not approach him. There was something about the way he smelled—an underlying suggestion of wildness—that puzzled me.

Jack returned with a tray of tea and biscuits and they chatted for a time, about the neighborhood, the weather, the recent rash of grave robbings, the killings. I watched them—two big men, the air of the predator about each—sipping their tea now and discussing the exotic flowers Talbot cultivated and how they might fare, even indoors, in this climate.

Then came a terrible crash from the attic.

I departed the room immediately, bounding up the stair, swinging around corners. Up another stair. . . .

The wardrobe doors were open. The Thing stood before it.

"Free!" it announced, flexing its limbs, furling and unfurling its dark, scaly wings. "Free!"

"Like hell!" I said, curling back my lips and leaping.

I caught it directly in the midsection, knocking it back into the wardrobe again. I slashed twice, left and right, as it sought to seize me. I dropped down and bit one of its legs. I roared and threw myself on it again, slashing faceward.

It drew back, retreating to the rear of its prison, leaving a heavy scent of musk in the air. I shouldered the doors shut, reared up, and tried to close the latch with my paw. Jack entered just then and did it for me. He held his knife loosely in his right hand.

"You are an exemplary watchdog, Snuff," he stated.

A moment later Larry Talbot came in.

"Problems?" he said. "Anything I can help with?"
The blade vanished before Jack turned.

"No, thank you," he said. "It was less serious than
it sounded. Shall we return to our tea?"

They departed.

I followed them down the stairs, Talbot moving as
silently as the master. I'd a feeling, somehow, that he
was in the Game, and that this incident had persuaded
him that we were, too. For as he was leaving he said,
"I see some busy days ahead, before this month is out.
If you ever need help—of any sort—you can count
on me."

Jack studied him for several long moments, then
replied, "Without even knowing my persuasion?"

"I think I know it," Talbot answered.

"How?"

"Good dog you've got there," Talbot said. "Knows
how to close a door."

Then he was gone. I followed him home, of course,
to see whether he really lived where he said he did.
When I saw that he did I had even more lines to
draw. Interesting ones now, though.

He never turned and looked back, yet I knew that
he could tell I was behind him all the way.

Later, I lay in the yard, drawing my lines. It had
become a much more complicated enterprise. Footsteps approached along the road, halted.

"Good dog," croaked an ancient voice. It was the
Druid. There followed a *plop* on the ground nearby,
as something he'd tossed over the garden wall landed.
"Good dog."

I rose and inspected it as he passed on along his
way. It was a piece of meat. Only the most wretched

of alley hounds might not have been wary. The thing reeked of exotic additives.

I picked it up carefully, bore it to a soft spot beneath a tree, dug a hole there, dropped it in, covered it.

"Bravo!" came a sibilant voice from above. "I didn't think you'd fall for that one."

I glanced up. Quicklime was coiled about a branch overhead.

"How long have you been there?" I asked.

"Since your first visitor came by—the big one. I'd been watching him. Is he in the Game?"

"I don't know. I think he may be, but it's hard to tell. He's a strange one. Doesn't seem to have a companion."

"Maybe he's his own best friend. Speaking of which—"

"Yes?"

"The crazy witch's companion may be running out of steam about now."

"What do you mean?"

" 'Ding, dong, dell.' "

"I don't follow you."

"Literally. Pussy's in the well."

"Who threw her in?"

"MacCab, full of sin."

"Where is it?"

"By the outhouse, full of shit. Back of Crazy Jill's place. Keeps it from going dry, I guess."

"Why tell me? You're the antisocial one."

"I've played before," he hissed. "I know it's too early in the Game to begin eliminating players. One should wait till after the death of the moon. MacCab and Morris are new at it, though."

I was on my feet and moving.

"Pussyfoot, pussyfoot. Wet, wet, wet," I heard him chanting as I ran off toward the hill.

I mounted the hill and raced down it toward Crazy Jill's, the landscape flowing to a blur about me. I pushed my way through a hedge when I reached her place, sought quickly, located the roofed and rock-girt structure, bucket on its rim. I ran to its side, rested my forepaws upon the ledge, and peered down into it. There was a faint splashing sound below.

"Gray!" I called.

A very faint "Here!" came to me.

"Get off to the side! I'm going to drop the bucket!" I called.

The splashing grew louder and faster.

I pushed the bucket off the ledge and listened to it wind down, heard it splash.

"Get in!" I called.

If you've ever tried turning a crank with your paws you know that it is rough work. It was a long, long while before I'd raised the bucket high enough for Graymalk to remove herself to the ledge. She stood there drenched and panting.

"How did you know?" she asked me.

"Quicklime saw it happen, felt the timing was bad, told me."

She shook herself, began licking her fur.

"Jill snatched a collection of Morris and MacCab's herbs," she said between licks. "Didn't go inside their place, though. They'd left them on their porch. Night-wind must have spotted us. Anything new?"

I told her about Bubo's visit last night, and Talbot's this morning.

"I'll go with you," she said. "Later. When I'm rested and dry. We'll check out the Count's crypt."

She shook herself again, licked again.

"In the meantime," she went on, "I need a warm place, and some catnappery."

"I'll see you later then. I have to check some things around the house."

"I'll come by."

I left her there near the outhouse. As I was making my way through the hedge, she called out, "By the way, thanks."

"*De nada*," I said, and I moved on up the hill.

October 9

LAST NIGHT WE OBTAINED MORE INGREDIENTS for the master's spell. As we paused on a corner in Soho the Great Detective and his companion came out of the fog and approached us.

"Good evening," he said.

"Good evening," Jack replied.

"Would you happen to have a light?"

Jack produced a package of wax vestas and passed it to him. Both men maintained eye contact as he lit his pipe.

"Lots of patrolmen about."

"Yes."

"Something's afoot, I daresay."

"I suppose so."

"It involves those killings, most likely."

"Yes, I'd say you're right."

He returned the matches.

The man had a strange way of regarding one's face, one's clothing, one's boots; and of listening.

45

As a watchdog, I could appreciate the mode of total attentiveness he assumed. It was not a normal human attitude. It was as if his entire being were concentrated in the moment, sensitive to every scrap of intelligence our encounter furnished.

"I've seen you about here other evenings."

"And I've seen you."

"Likely we'll meet again."

"You may be right."

"In the meantime, take care. It's become dangerous."

"Watch out for yourself, also."

"Oh, I will. Good night."

"Good night."

I had refrained from growling lightly for effect, though the thought had passed through my mind. I listened to their footsteps long after they had gone from sight.

"Snuff," Jack said, "remember that man."

Somewhere on the long, long walk home an owl passed us, riding the chill breezes on motionless wings. I could not tell whether it was Nightwind. There were rats about the bridge, and I did not know whether Bubo was one of them. Stars swam in the Thames, and the air was full of dirty smells.

I kept pace with Jack's long strides while investigating every sleeping street person huddled in every shelter along our way. I felt at times as if we were being followed, but could discover no reason for my apprehension. It could well be that our mere progress through October was in itself sufficient to produce anxiety. Things, of course, would continue to worsen before they got better—if they were ever to get better again.

"Ah, Jack," came a voice from our left. "Good evening."

Jack halted and turned, his hand near to the place where his knife was concealed.

Larry Talbot stepped out of the shadows, touching the brim of his hat.

"Mr. Talbot . . ." Jack began.

" 'Larry,' please."

"That's right, you're American. Larry, good evening. What are you doing out so late?"

"Walking. It seemed a good night for it. I tend to insomnia. You were in town perhaps?"

"Yes."

"So was I. I met the Great Detective himself, and his friend. He stopped to ask me for a light."

"Oh?"

Larry glanced at his palm, seemed reassured of something, went on: "I got the impression he's involved in the investigation of the recent slayings . . . of which I understand there was another tonight. You hear anything about it?"

"No."

"Cautioned me to watch my step. I guess that's good advice for all of us, though."

"Did he give the impression he had any real clues?"

Larry shook his head.

"He's a hard man to read. His partner muttered something about dogs, though."

"Interesting."

"I'll walk you partway back, if I may."

"Surely."

"Eight days more till the death of the moon," Jack said after a time. "Are you a moon-watcher, Larry?"

"Very much so," came the reply.

"I'd guessed that."

We walked for a long while in silence, Larry's stride matching Jack's own.

"Are you acquainted with the one called the Count?" Larry asked suddenly.

Jack was silent for several paces, then said slowly, "I've heard of him, but I've never had the pleasure."

"Well, he's come to town," Larry said. "He and I go back a long way. I can always tell when he's about. Opener, I'd guess."

Jack was silent again. In my mind, I revisited yesterday afternoon, when Graymalk and I had made our way along the route Bubo had shown me. She ventured into the crypt while I waited above. She was down there a long while, silent as a cat, before she repaired topside.

"Yes," she told me then, "the rat was right. There's a rather handsome coffin down there, up on a pair of trestles. And an opened trunk containing changes of clothes and some personal items."

"No mirror?"

"No mirror. And Needle's hung himself amid the roots overhead."

"I guess Bubo traded fair," I said.

"Never trust a rat," she told me. "You said he'd sneaked into your place and was snooping around. Supposing that was his real reason for being there, and he only offered to trade information to cover it over when you caught him?"

"I'd thought of that," I said. "But I heard him come in, and I know just where he was. All he got to see was the Things in the Mirror."

"Things in the Mirror?"

"Yes. Don't you have any?"

"Afraid not. What do they do?"

"Slither."

"Oh."

"Come on. I'll show you."

"You sure it's all right?"

"Yes."

Later, she placed a paw against its reflection as she stared.

"You're right," she said. "They—slither."

"Change colors, too, when they get excited."

"Where did you get them?"

"Deserted village in India. Everybody'd died of plague or run away from it."

"They must have a use. . . ."

"Yes, they're sticky."

"Oh."

I walked her back to Jill's, where she said, "I can't invite you in, or show you any of our stuff, I'm afraid."

"That's okay."

"Will you be prowling tonight?"

"Have to go into town."

"Good luck."

"Thanks."

Jack and I parted from Larry at the crossroads near his place and headed west toward our own. When we came into the yard, I smelled owl and saw Nightwind perched in the same tree Quicklime had visited. I growled a "good evening" but he did not return it. I rushed inside first in the event he was a lookout, but there was no one there and there were no odors of intruders. And everything was as it should be. Just simple spying, then. When there's nothing else to do, we watch each other.

Jack went off to deal with his acquisition. I did dognappery in the parlor.

October 10

IT RAINED STEADILY ALL DAY, SO I DIDN'T GO out much. And not far when I did. No one came by.

I made the rounds many more times than usual, partly out of boredom. Good thing that I did.

The Thing was strangely quiet as I entered the basement. In a moment, I saw why. We had developed a leak. The water entered at the wall, ran along a sagging beam, and dripped down several feet farther in. It had formed a puddle, and the puddle was slowly spreading. One moist pseudopod was extended in the direction of the Circle, having perhaps another ten inches to run before it breached it.

I howled, a long, loud, mournful thing I saved for occasions such as this. Then I threw myself onto the streamer and rolled in it, absorbing it into my coat.

"Hey!" cried the Thing. "Cut that out! This was meant to be!"

"So was this!" I snapped, and I turned over and rolled in the puddle itself, soaking myself as I tossed and wriggled, absorbing a great deal.

I moved off to a far, dry corner then and turned over several times on the floor there, spreading the moisture about in a place where it would evaporate harmlessly.

"Damn dog!" it snarled. "Another few minutes and I'd've made it!"

"I guess it's just not your lucky day," I replied.

There were footsteps on the stair.

When Jack entered and saw what had happened, he went and fetched a mop. Shortly, he was cleaning up the rest of the puddle and wringing it out into a basin, while the Thing fumed and turned pink, blue, and sickly green. He set a pail beneath the drip then and told me to call him again if we developed any other leaks.

We didn't, though. I checked regularly all afternoon. The rain finally stopped after dark, and I waited several hours after that—just to be sure—before going out.

Moving around to the front of the house, I unearthed the now slimy piece of drugged meat from where I had buried it. I carried it up the road with me and deposited it in plain sight at Owen's front door. The place was dark and Cheeter was nowhere in sight, so I prowled around a bit.

Under the huge old oak in the back I discovered eight large wicker baskets in various stages of construction, and seven smaller ones. There were also lots of heavy ropes about.

I sniffed around. There was also a ladder nearby. Such industry, for a frail-looking old guy. . . .

I walked a straight line then, passing through yard and field. Partway to my goal it began raining again, lightly. A huge mass of clouds occluded a small area of sky, darker shapes within darkness, and there came a brief, pale glow from within followed by a low rumble of thunder.

Continuing, I came at last into the precincts of the Good Doctor's abode. It was as if I were directly beneath the low cloud-cluster now; and even as I watched, a triple-pronged piece of brightness fell from overhead to dance among the rods on the old building's roof. The crash came almost immediately and the basement windows blazed more brightly.

I remained in the grasses, listening, and I heard a man's voice from within shouting something about seeing to the Leydens. There followed another flash-crash, another devil's tap dance of fire on the roof, more shouts, more flares from the windows. I crept nearer.

Peeking in, I could see a tall man in a white coat—his back to me—leaning over something on a long table, his own form blocking my view of his subject. A small, misshapen individual crouched in a far corner, eyes darting, making nervous movements with his hands. There came another flash, another crash. Electrical discharges played about a bank of equipment off to the tall man's right. They stained my eyes with afterimages for a time. The tall man shouted something and moved to one side, the small man rose and began to dance about. Something on the table—covered, I could now see, by a sheet—twitched. It might have been a large leg that did it, beneath the cloth. There came another blinding burst and a deafening roar. The scene within was momentarily an inferno. Through it all, it seemed to me that something large and manlike tried for a moment to sit up on the table, its exact outline masked by the flowing cloth.

I backed away. I turned and ran as more fire fell from the heavens. I had done my duty. This seemed ample investigation here for one night.

I walked my next line from the Good Doctor's to Larry Talbot's place. I came out of the rain partway there and shook myself at some point. When I reached Larry's house I saw it to be well lighted. Perhaps he really did suffer from insomnia.

Circling the place many times, I spiraled inward, pausing to inspect a small gazebo to the rear. Within, outlined in dried mud, I discovered a large paw-print which appeared identical to the one I had found near my home.

Drawing nearer, I rose onto my hind legs, forepaws against the side of the house, and peered in through a window. Empty room. The third one I inspected let upon a skylighted room filled with plants. Larry was there, staring into the depths of an enormous flower and smiling. His lips were moving, and though I could hear low sounds, I could not distinguish the words he uttered. The huge blossom moved before him, whether because of air currents or by its own volition I could not tell. He continued to murmur, and finally I turned away. Lots of people talk to their plants.

Next, I oriented myself as best I could and attempted to follow a straight line from Larry's place to the Count's crypt. I came to the ruined church first, and I paused there, trying to visualize the rest of the pattern. By then, a faint lightening had begun in the east.

As I lay puzzling, a large bat—much bigger than Needle—swooped in from the north, passing behind a big tree. It did not emerge on the tree's other side, however. Instead, I heard the softest of footfalls, and a dark-suited man in a black cloak stepped out from behind the tree.

I stared. His head snapped in my direction, and he spoke: "Who is there?"

Suddenly, I felt very exposed. There was only one role I could think to play.

Uttering an idiot series of yips, I rushed forward, wagging my tail furiously, and threw myself on the ground before him, rolling about like some attention-starved stray.

His bright lips twitched into a brief, small smile. Then he leaned forward and scratched me behind the ears.

"Good dog," he said, in slow, guttural tones.

Then he patted my head, straightened, and walked off toward the crypt. He halted when he reached it. One moment he was standing there, the next moment he was gone.

I decided it was time to get gone myself. His touch had been very cold.

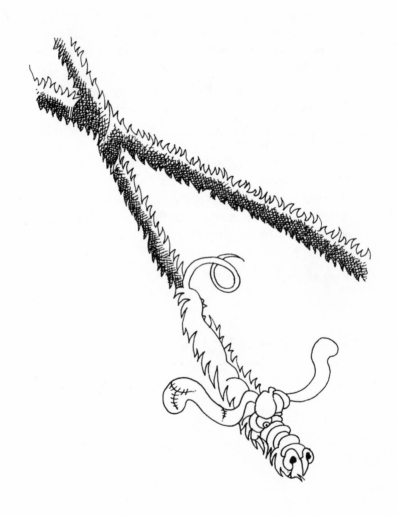

October 11

BRISK MORNING. AFTER I MADE MY ROUNDS I went outside. I could discover nothing untoward, so I set off in the direction of the Good Doctor's place. As I was trotting along the road, however, I heard a familiar voice from a small grove to my right:

"That, sir, is the same dog," it said.

"How can you be sure?" came the response.

"I noted the markings, and his are identical. Also, he has the same limp in his left foreleg, the same shredded right ear. . . ."

. . . Old war injuries—disagreement with a mindless guy in the West Indies—long ago. . . .

It was the Great Detective and his companion who had spoken, of course.

"Here's a good fellow," he said. "Good dog. Good dog."

I remembered my act of the previous evening, wagged my tail, and tried to look friendly.

"Good dog," he repeated. "Show us where you live. Take us home."

He patted my head as he said it, his hands being much warmer than the last friendly fellow's I'd met.

"Home. Go home now."

Thinking of Graymalk in the well, I led them to Morris and MacCab's place. I waited with them on the porch till I heard footsteps approaching inside in response to their knocking. Then I withdrew and cut a straight line from there to the Count's crypt. The results were interesting; and even more so when I ran in a line from there to the Good Doctor's.

I did several more thereafter, confirming my results.

October 12

LOW DAY. THE THING IN THE CIRCLE TRIED
being a greyhound. I was never attracted to skinny
ladies, though. Growled a few times at the Thing in
the Attic. Watched the slitherers. Watched Jack as
he puttered with his acquisitions. It was still too early
for him actually to start using them.

Heard from Graymalk later that Nightwind had
seized Quicklime and borne him far out over the
Thames and dropped him in. He was washed ashore
later. Spent a long time slithering back. Not sure what
they'd been arguing about.

Also learned of several cases of sudden severe
anemia among the neighbors. I'm glad the Count
doesn't do dogs.

I took Jack his slippers this evening and lay at his feet
before a roaring fire while he smoked his pipe, sipped
sherry, and read the newspaper. He read aloud everything involving killings, arsons, mutilations, grave
robberies, church desecrations, and unusual thefts. It
is very pleasant just being domestic sometimes.

October 13

THE GREAT DETECTIVE WAS BACK TODAY. I glimpsed him only briefly from a hedgerow where I was burying something. He did not see me.

Later, Graymalk told me that he had visited Owen's place. Owen and Cheeter were out, and he had looked about some, discovering the wicker baskets. His assistant injured his wrist, she said, having been sent up the ladder into the oak to test the strength of some branches, whence he had fallen. Fortunately, he landed on a heap of mistletoe, or it might have been worse.

That evening, I heard a scraping at an upstairs window while I was making my rounds. I went to it and peered out. At first I saw nothing, then I realized that a small form was darting back and forth.

"Snuff! Let me in! Help!" it cried.

It was Needle.

"I know better than to invite you guys inside," I said.

"That's the boss! I'm just a bat! I don't even like tomato juice! Please!"

"What's wrong?"

I heard a loud *thunk* from the other side of the wall.

"It's the vicar!" he cried. "He's wigged out! Let me in!"

I undid the latch with my paw and pushed. It opened a few inches, and he was inside. He fell to the floor, panting. There followed another *thunk* from without.

"I won't forget this, Snuff," he said. "Give me a minute. . . ."

I gave him two, then he stirred.

"Got any bugs about?" he asked. "I've got this fast metabolism, and I've been getting a lot of exercise."

"It'd take a lot of effort catching them," I said. "They're pretty fast. How about some fruit?"

"Fruit is good, too. . . ."

"There's a bowl in the kitchen."

He was too tired to fly it, though, and I was afraid he was too fragile to pick up in my mouth. So I let him cling to my fur.

As I walked downstairs, he repeated, "Wigged out, wigged out. . . ."

"Tell me about it," I said, as he feasted on a plum and two grapes.

"Vicar Roberts has become convinced there's something unnatural in the neighborhood," he said.

"How strange. What might have led him to that belief?"

"The bodies with no blood left in them, and the

people with anemia—who all seem to have had vivid dreams involving bats. Things like that."

I'd seen Vicar Roberts many times on my rambles—a fat little man, dundrearied, and wearing old-fashioned, square-lensed, gold-framed spectacles. I'd been told that he often grew very red of complexion at the high points of sermons, splattering little droplets of spittle about, and that he was sometimes given to fits of twitchings followed by unconsciousness and strange transports.

"It is understandable in someone of an hysterical personality type," I said.

"I suppose so. At any rate, he recently took to running about the parish by night, armed with a crossbow and a quiver of bolts—'flying stakes,' he calls them. I hear your door! I'll bet that's him! Hide me!"

"No need," I said. "The master would not let an obvious madman armed with a dangerous weapon come in and search the house. This is a place of peace and refinement."

The door was opened and I heard them speak quietly. Then the vicar's voice was raised. Jack, being a gentleman, responded in his usual soft, courteous tone. The vicar began to shout about Creatures of the Night and Unholy Practices and Living Blasphemies and Things Like That.

"You gave it sanctuary!" I heard him cry. "I'm coming after it!"

"You are not," Jack responded.

"I've a moral warrant, and I bloody well am!" said the vicar.

Then I heard the sounds of a scuffle.

"Excuse me, Needle," I said.

"Of course, Snuff."

I ran on into the front hallway, but Jack had already closed and bolted the door. He smiled when he saw me. There came a pounding from behind him.

"It's all right, Snuff," he said. "I'm not about to set the dogs on the poor fellow. Uh—Where *is* your friend, anyway?"

I glanced toward the kitchen.

He walked that way, preceding me by several paces. When I entered he was already feeding a grape to Needle.

" 'Creature of the Night,' " he said. " 'Living Blasphemy.' You're safe here. You can even have a peach if you'd like."

He strolled off, whistling. The pounding on the front door continued for another minute or so, then stopped.

"What's to be done about that man, d'you think?" Needle asked.

"Stay out of his way, I guess."

"Easy to say. He took a shot at Nightwind yesterday, and a couple at Cheeter recently."

"Why? They're not into sanguinary stuff."

"No, but he also claims to have had a vision concerning a society of wretched individuals and their familiars preparing for some big psychic event which will place them at odds with each other and threaten the safety of humanity. The vampire business was the first 'sign,' as he put it, that this was true."

"I wonder what busybody sent him that vision?"

"Hard to guess," Needle said. "But he could be shooting at you, or Jack, tomorrow."

"Perhaps the parishioners will send him to the

Continent," I said, "to take the waters at some salubrious spa. We only need about two and a half weeks more."

"I doubt they will. In fact, I think he's enlisted some of them in the cause of his vision. He wasn't the only one out there with a crossbow tonight."

"Then I think we're going to have to identify those people, find out where they live, and keep an eye open in their direction."

"I use echolocation myself, but I get the idea."

"Nightwind and Cheeter obviously already know. I'll tell Graymalk if you'll tell Quicklime and Bubo."

"What about that Talbot fellow?"

"So far as I can tell, Larry Talbot doesn't have a nonvegetable companion. He can take care of himself, I think."

"All right."

". . . And we should all agree to spread the word on who they are and where they live. It won't matter to someone like that what your persuasion is."

"I agree with you on this."

Later, I checked around outside and there were no crossbow-persons in the vicinity. So I opened the window again and let Needle out, the vicar's quarrels stuck in the siding over our heads.

October 14

RAYMALK HAD JUST FINISHED DIGGING
something up and was dragging it to the house when
I entered her yard. I brought her up to date on last
night's events, and while she cautioned me never to
trust a bat she acknowledged the seriousness of the
threat presented by the vicar and his crew. Someone
had apparently taken a shot at them from the top of a
hill as she and Jill passed overhead last night, causing
them to veer and experience an exciting moment or
two near a chimney.

When she had completed her task, Graymalk said,
"There were a couple of things I wanted to talk to
you about."

"Go ahead."

"First things first, then. I'd better show you this
one."

I followed her out of the yard.

"A London police officer visited Constable Terence

yesterday," she said. "Quicklime and I saw him go by on a chestnut mare."

"Yes?"

"Later, Cheeter saw the mare browsing in a field and mentioned it as something odd. We sought about the area but the rider was nowhere near. After a time, we went away."

"You should have gotten me. I could have backtracked."

"I came by. But you weren't around."

"I did have some chores. . . . Anyway, what happened?"

"I was in another field later—the place we're going to now, near you. There was a pair of crows rising and falling there, and I was thinking of lunch. So were they, as it turned out. They were eating the officer's eyes, where he lay in a clump of weeds. Just up ahead."

We approached. The birds were gone. So were the eyes. The man was in uniform. His throat had been cut.

I sat down and stared.

"I don't like this at all," I finally said.

"Didn't think you would."

"It's too near. We live just over that way."

"And we live over there."

"Have you told anyone else yet?"

"No. So it's not one of yours—unless you're a very good actor."

I shook my head.

"It doesn't make any sense."

"Jack *is* supposed to have magical control over a certain ritual blade."

"And Owen has a sickle. So what? And Rastov has an amazing icon drawn by a mad Arab who'd given up on Islam. But he could have used a kitchen knife. And Jill has her broom. She could still find something to cut a throat with."

"You know about the icon!"

"Sure. It's my job—keeping track of the tools. I'm a watcher, remember? And the Count probably has the ring, and the Good Doctor the bowl. I think it's just a regular killing. But now we're stuck with a body in the neighborhood—and not just *any* body. It's a policeman. There'll be an investigation, and—face it—we're all suspicious characters with things to hide. We only planned to be here for a few weeks. We do as much as we can of the active stuff outside the area, for now. We try to stay relatively inconspicuous here. But we're all transients with strange histories. This is going to spoil a lot of planning."

"If the body is found."

"Yes."

"Couldn't you dig a hole, push it in, and cover it up? The way you do with bones—only bigger?"

"They'd spot a new grave, once they start looking. No. We have to get it out of here."

"You're big enough to drag it. Could you get it to that ruined church, push it down the opening?"

"Still too near. And it might scare the Count into moving, for fear people will be poking around there."

"So?"

"I like knowing where he is. If he moves, we'll have to find him again. . . ."

"The body," she said, interrupting an intriguing chain of speculation.

"Yes, I'm thinking. It's awfully far to the river, but I'm wondering whether I might be able to drag it there in stages and push it in. There are a lot of places I could stow it along the way. . . ."

"What about the horse?"

"Could you check with Quicklime? Tell him what happened, give him our reasoning. Horses are often afraid of snakes. Perhaps he could scare him into running back to town."

"It sounds worth a try. Maybe you'd better check to be sure you can handle the body."

I moved around to the rear, seized hold of the collar, braced my legs, and pulled. He came along nicely over the damp grass. A little lighter than he looked, too.

"Yes, I can move him. I know I can't take him all the way at once, but at least I can get him out of here."

"Good, I'll go and see whether Quicklime is out and about."

She dashed off, and I commenced pulling the officer along, his ruined face toward a clouded sky. All afternoon, I dragged and rested, hiding him twice, once when people were about, another time to return home and make my rounds. And the Thing in the Steamer Trunk was acting up again. At one point, the horse did trot by, along the roadside.

I was bushed by evening and returned home to nap and eat, leaving the corpse in a copse. I wasn't even halfway there yet.

October 15

CONTINUING GRAY AND DRIZZLING. I MADE my rounds and got out early to check about the house. I'd gotten out several times during the night to move things a little farther along. I was bone-weary that morning, and Needle came by at dawn.

"He was out again with his crossbow crew," he reported. "I'm still not sure how many there are, but I can show you where one lives."

"Later," I said. "I'm very busy."

"All right," he replied. "Show you this evening, if we're both free."

"Any word on the police?"

"Police? What about?"

"Never mind. I'll tell you when I see you later. Unless someone else does it first."

"Till then," he said, and he darted off.

I went and dragged the corpse till I couldn't manage another step. Then I dragged myself home, jaws aching, paws sore, my old injury from the zombie affair acting up.

While I was resting under the tree Graymalk came by.

"How's it going?" she asked.

"Pretty fair," I answered. "I still have a long way to go, but he's stashed safe enough. I saw the horse go by. I gathered you took care of things."

"Yes, Quicklime was very cooperative. You should have seen his routine. The horse was quite impressed."

"Good. Has anyone been by?"

"Yes. I watched the constable's place earlier. An inspector was by there from the city. So were the Great Detective and his companion, whose wrist was bandaged."

"Poor fellow. Did they stay long?"

"Not the inspector. But the Detective stayed to visit the vicar, and several others."

"Oh my! I wonder what he told them?"

"I wasn't in a position to hear. But the Detective did considerable strolling about the neighborhood afterwards. They even went somewhat afield toward the Good Doctor's place."

"Didn't go off in the Count's direction, did they?"

"No. They stopped and asked Owen about bee-keeping, though. A pretext, of course. And I was near when they noted the arrows stuck in the side of your house."

"Damn!" I said. "Forgot. Have to do something about them."

"I have to go bury some things now," she said. "I'll try to talk to you again later."

"Yes. I have some work, too."

I made my rounds again, then went off to drag the inspector a little farther along. Having done it both ways, they're easier when they're stiff than when they're limp, and he was limp again.

Evening. Jack wanted to go out again. When it gets to this point in the game there are always a few last-minute items on the shopping list. This time the place was swarming with patrolmen, some of them walking in pairs. Crazy Jill swooshed by at one point, turning a few heads; through the opened door of a gin mill I saw Rastov seated at a table, alone, save for a bottle of vodka and a glass (I wondered what happened to Quicklime on these occasions, if he's gone internal); a rat resembling Bubo scurried by, a finger in his mouth; Owen went staggering past with a pair of fellows, faces streaked with coal dust, singing something incomprehensible in Welsh; I saw Morris, bewigged, dressed like a woman, heavily rouged, hanging onto MacCab's arm.

"Party time," Jack observed, "before things start to get serious."

An eyepatched man with shaggy hair, a terrible limp, and a withered hand staggered by, selling pencils from a tin cup. I went on point even before he emerged from the fog, recognizing from the scent that it was the Great Detective in disguise. Jack bought a pencil from him and paid him handsomely for it.

He muttered a "Bless you, guv'nor" and limped off.

Our quest was extremely difficult this time, and I must say the master took unusual chances. As we were fleeing, a number of patrolmen in pursuit, whistles ablare, a door opened to our left and a familiar voice said, "In here!"

We ducked inside, the door was closed softly behind us, and moments later I heard the police rush past.

"Thanks," I heard Jack whisper.

"Glad to be able to help," Larry replied. "Every-body seems to be out tonight."

"It's getting to be that time," Jack said, and his parcel began to drip softly.

"I've a towel here that you can have," Larry said.

"Thank you. How'd you know it might be needed?"

"I've a way of anticipating things," Larry replied.

He did not accompany us back this time, and I excused myself shortly after the bridge to return to the corpse and drag it farther. Something had gotten to it and stolen a few nibbles, but it was still largely intact.

As I was struggling along I thought I heard Graymalk voice a greeting from somewhere over-head, but my mouth was full and I did not want to stop work to look up.

October 16

I SLEPT AWFULLY WELL LAST NIGHT, AWOKE aching, and made the rounds.

"How's about an Afghan?" the Thing in the Circle asked, having assumed that lovely, aristocratic form.

"Sorry. Too tired today," I responded.

It cursed and I departed.

The slitherers were all clustered, bluely, at one point, and I could not figure why. One of life's small mysteries. . . .

Outside, I found a dead bat nailed to the tree by a crossbow bolt. It wasn't Needle, just some civilian. Something would have to be done. . . .

I made my way back to the body, which had a few more parts missing and didn't smell too good, and dragged it to the next place of concealment. But my heart just wasn't in it. I could go no farther. I turned and walked home, jaws sore, neck aching, paws tender.

"I want to die. I want to die," came a small voice almost from underfoot.

"Quicklime, what's the matter?" I asked.

"The master was sick right here," he said. "I took advantage and got out. I want to die."

"Keep lying in the road and some cart will come along and give you your wish. Better get over to the side. Here, I'll help."

I carried the ailing reptile into the brush.

"What should I do, Snuff?" he asked.

"Lie in the sun and sweat it out," I told him. "Drink lots of liquids."

"I don't know if it's worth it."

"You'll feel better later. Trust me."

I left him moaning atop a rock. I went on home, entered, and dragged myself through my rounds. The master was not in. I went and slept in the parlor, woke and ate, dozed again.

Later, I heard Jack's footsteps approaching the front door. He was accompanied, I knew from the footfalls, by Larry Talbot. They halted outside, continuing a discussion which must have been ongoing as they'd walked. It seemed they had just come from Constable Terence's office, where they'd been invited, in the company of a number of other neighbors, for questioning by city police concerning the missing officer I'd been dragging through fields. I gathered that another neighborhood group had followed them in, to continue the investigation. So far as I felt just then, they could have what was left of the man.

". . . And Vicar Roberts, sitting there, glaring at everyone—as if we'd *all* done it," Larry was saying. "What right had that man at an official investigation?

He's more than a little dotty."

"Fortunately," Jack responded. "Otherwise, some-one might pay more heed to his notions."

"True," Larry said. "If anyone had to be done in, he'd seem the best choice."

"Then they would give some credence to his vision."

"Of course." There followed a sigh. "I'm just venting a little spleen at those who make diffi-cult things more difficult." He sighed again. Then, "I noted he hadn't his crossbow with him," he added.

"Now *that* would have raised a few eyebrows."

They both chuckled.

"Larry," Jack said suddenly. "I confess that I real-ly don't understand your part in this. That you are knowledgeable is obvious, that you know what you are doing, I am certain, and that you've been help-ful, I can't deny. And I am grateful for it. But you haven't apparently been collecting the items neces-sary to assemble a structure of power to be focused one way or the other. Now, I admit that when you came out that first day and as much as proclaimed yourself a closer, I thought it a bit gauche. But even that, I suspect now, had a method to it. Still, so far as I can tell, you have done nothing that would further that end, let alone assemble defenses against the days ahead. If this be true, you are inviting disaster by announcing affiliation and continuing to reside in the precincts of the Game."

"You are the only one I've told, Jack," Larry replied.

"Why?"

"I've met most of the others, of course. But there was something about you—perhaps it had to do with the dog—that assured me I was safe in revealing my persuasion. I've told you that anticipation is my *forte*."

"But your role in things, sir! What is it?"

"I never tell anybody everything. It might influence their actions and affect those things I've anticipated. Then I'd have to start over again, and it might be too late."

"I confess you've almost lost me, but I can feel some rationale behind your words. Tell me what you would then, when you would."

"Assuredly."

I heard their palms strike together as they clasped hands, then Larry's retreating footsteps.

Later, I went back to drag things along a little farther. I'd come to a place where the ground was mushy, and it was awful. He kept catching on brambles and getting knotted up in fallen branches and stuck between hillocks. He may have lost a few pieces in that area but I was too tired to look. Finally, I just gave up and went home. It was near noon, and chances were we'd be going out again that night, it being the Eve and all. I needed my rest.

On the way back, I looked for Quicklime on his stone, but he was nowhere in sight. There was a very twisty trail leading away, though.

Graymalk was waiting on the tree's most popular branch, on my return. I noted that the pierced bat was missing, though the quarrel was still in place.

"Snuff," she asked, climbing down, "have you done it yet?"

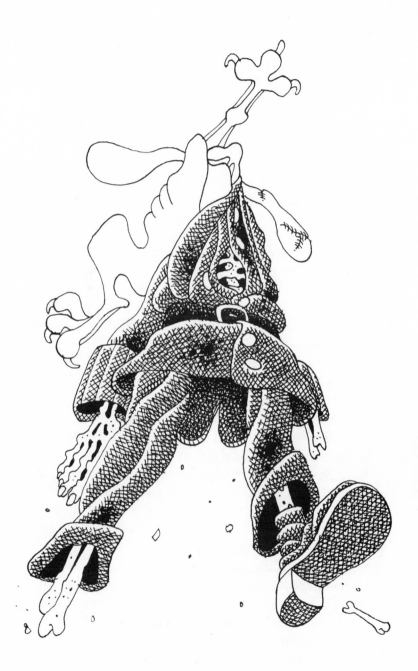

"Don't ask me," I said. "This is proving a major undertaking."

"I'm sorry," she said, "but I was at the constable's this morning with the mistress, and I heard all the talk—"

"What did they say?"

"That they knew he came here and they know he didn't come back, and they won't leave a horse pie unturned till they find him or know what happened to him. Things like that."

"Oh. Nothing new. How did the questioning go?"

"Fine, with us. The mistress did her crazy act and talked about him being carried off by fairies for a changeling. They had to ask her to be still. Rastov suddenly understood a lot less English than he used to. Morris and MacCab were very polite and said they knew nothing. Jack was quite urbane and seemed very sympathetic but also had nothing to add. The Good Doctor was indignant that the quiet hamlet he'd sought to do his research should suddenly be violated by things he'd wanted to get away from. Larry Talbot said he'd never seen the man. Owen said that they'd talked but he hadn't seen him again after that, and didn't know where he'd gone after he'd left him. He may have been the last to see him, though, according to a rough schedule the officer'd mentioned to the constable."

"What of the vicar?"

"He just said that someone was lying, to cover the Devil's work, and he'd find out who."

I rolled in a dry patch of grass and removed a thorn with my teeth.

"So how far along are you?" she asked.

"Perhaps two-thirds of the way. I've come to a bad area."

"They'll likely search around here first, then work their way outwards. So you should still have some time."

"That's a comfort. You going out tonight?"

"Probably."

"Tomorrow it dies. No hard feelings, however things go."

"No."

"I found a big patch of catnip on my way to the river. If we both get through this, I'll buy you a drink."

"Thanks."

She stretched. I stretched and yawned. We nodded to each other and went our ways.

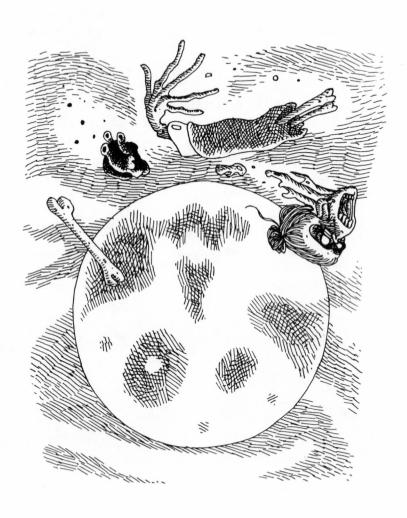

October 17

OON IT BEGINS. TODAY IS THE DAY OF THE New Moon. The power will rise till the night of its fullness, on the thirty-first, the combination which brings us together. And with the rising we begin our work, that which draws us apart. The days ahead will be interesting, as the openers and closers reveal themselves by their actions. Last night may have represented a final act of cooperation.

Jack wanted to visit a cemetery for a few final ingredients. He decided upon a distant, isolated one we had been to once before. He went on horseback, bearing a spade and bull's-eye lantern, and I trotted along beside.

He tethered his horse amid some trees outside the graveyard, and we went in on foot. It was, of course, a very dark night. But with the aid of the lantern we quickly located an appropriately secluded plot of recent turning. Jack set to work immediately, and I went about my watching.

It was a pleasantly mild evening for October, with a few bats flitting by, bright stars overhead. I heard footsteps in the distance, but they were not headed in our direction and I saw no cause for alarm. I patrolled our small area in an almost leisurely fashion. After a time, something very large passed overhead, descending. It did not land nearby, however, nor make any movement to approach us. A bit later, something equally large passed—again, descending, though in a different area than the first, and, again, making no overtures toward us—and I remained alert but voiced no warning. I heard horses on the trail a little after that, sounds of dismounting, more footsteps. Later, a wagon creaked to a halt, and I heard its brake being set. The sounds of a few whispered voices reached me then, from various distant areas. I began to feel uncomfortable at all this activity. I patrolled farther afield; and, listening closely, I began hearing the sounds of spades from many directions.

"I remember you," came a faintly familiar voice. "You're a watchdog, like me, with big teeth."

It was the graveyard dog, making his rounds.

" 'Evening," I said. "Yes, I recall. Seems to be a lot of activity all of a sudden."

"Too much," he replied. "I'm not sure I care to give the alarm. Might get mobbed. After all, everybody here is dead, so who cares? They won't complain. The older I get the more conservative I feel. I'm just not much into heavy action these days. I do wish everybody'd fill up their holes neatly, though, afterwards. Maybe you could pass the word along?"

"I don't know," I said. "I don't know who all's

out there. It's not like a trade union, you know, with operating rules and policies. We usually just get the work done as efficiently as possible and get the hell out."

"Well, it would be nice if you cleaned up after yourselves. Less trouble for me."

"I'm afraid I can only speak for the master, but he's usually quite neat in these matters. Maybe you'd better approach a few of the others yourself."

"I'm inclined to let it go by," he said. "Too bad."

We strolled around a bit together then. Later, a voice very like MacCab's called out from down the hill, "Damn! I need a left femur and this one ain't got one!"

"Left femur, you say?" came an ancient croaking voice from nearby, which could have been Owen's. "I've one right here I ain't usin'. Have you a liver, though? That's my need."

"Easily done!" came the reply. "Bide a moment. There! Trade?"

"You have it! Catch!"

Something flashed through the air to rattle farther down the hill, followed by scurrying sounds.

"Fair enough! Here's yer liver!"

There came a *splap* from higher up and a muttered "Got it!"

"Hey!" came a lady's voice then, from off to the left. "While you're about it, have you a skull?"

"Indeed I do!" said the second man. "What'll you give?"

"What do you need?"

"Fingerbones!"

"Done! I'll tie 'em together with a piece of twine!"

"Here's your skull!"

"Got it! Yours'll be along shortly!"

"Has anyone the broken vertebrae of a hanged man?" came a deep masculine voice with a Hungarian accent, from somewhere far to the right.

There followed a minute's silence. Then, "I've some mashed ones here! Dunno how they got that way, though!"

"Perhaps they'll do. Send them along, please!"

Something white and rattling flashed through the starlit air.

"Yes. I can work with these. What'll you have for them?"

"They're on the house! I'm done! 'Night!"

There followed the sounds of rapidly retreating footfalls.

"See?" the old dog said. "He didn't fill it in."

"I'm sorry."

"I'll be up kicking dirt all night."

"Afraid I can't help you. I've got my own job to see to."

"Eyeballs, anyone?" came a call.

"Over here," said someone with a Russian accent. "One of them, please."

"I'll have the other," came an aristocratic voice from the opposite direction.

"Either of you got a couple of floating ribs, or a pair of kidneys?"

"Down here, on the kidneys!" came a new voice. "And I'm in need of a patella!"

"What's that?"

"Knee bone!"

"Oh? No problem. . . ."

On the way out, we passed a white-bearded, frail-looking man, half-adoze, leaning on a spade near the gate. Casual inspection would have had one believe him a sexton, out for a bit of night air, but his scent was that of the Great Detective, hardly drowsing. Someone had obviously spoken too publicly.

Jack muffled himself and we slunk by, shadows amid shadows.

Thus was all our work quickly concluded to everyone's satisfaction, save for the tired hound. Such times are rare, such times are fleeting, but always bright when caught, measured, hung, and later regarded in times of adversity, there in the kinder halls of memory, against the flapping of the flames.

Forgive me. The New Moon, as they say, gives rise to reflection. Time to make my rounds. Then some more dragging.

October 18

FIRST TIME OUT YESTERDAY I GOT HIM farther through the muck, but he was still in it when I left him. I was tired. Jack was sequestered with his objects. The police were about, searching the area. The vicar was out, too, offering exhortations to the searchers. Night came on, and later I made my way back to the muck, chasing off a few vermin and beginning the long haul once again.

I'd worked on and off for over an hour, allowing myself several panting breaks, when I realized I was no longer alone. He was bigger than me even, and he moved with a silence I envied—some piece of the night cut loose and drifting against lesser blacknesses. He seemed to know the moment I became aware of him, and he moved toward me with a long, effortless stride, one of the largest dogs I'd ever seen outside of Ireland.

Correction. As he came on I realized he wasn't

really a dog. It was a great gray wolf that was bearing down on me. I quickly reviewed my knowledge of the submissive postures these guys are into as I backed away from the corpse.

"You can have it," I said. "It's all right with me. It's not in the best of shape, though."

He loomed nearer. Monstrous jaws, great feral eyes. . . . Then he sat down.

"So this is where it is," he said.

"What?"

"The missing body. Snuff, you are tampering with evidence."

"And you might say I'm tampering with something already tampered with. Who are you?"

"Larry. Talbot."

"Could've fooled me. I thought you were—a great wolf . . . oh."

"That, too."

"*Were*, huh? And you're shifted. But this is the dark of the moon."

"So it is."

"Neat trick, that. How'd you manage it?"

"I can do it whenever I choose, with certain botanical aids, and retain full rationality—save when the moon is full. It's only involuntary then, with certain unfortunate accompaniments."

"So I understand. Like, berserk."

"*Wulfsark*," he said. "Yes."

"So why are you here?"

"I tracked you. Ordinarily, this is my favorite time of month, without a trace of moon to disturb me. But I forsook this to do some investigating. Then it became necessary that I speak with you. So I came

looking. What are you doing with the body, anyway?"

"I was trying to get it to the river, where I want to
drop it in. Someone had left it near our place, and I
was afraid Jack would be suspected."

"I'll give you a ha— I'll help."

With that, he seized it by a shoulder and began
walking backwards. No bracing himself and tugging,
the way I'd had to manage it. He just kept walking,
picking up speed, even. I didn't see any way I could
help. I'd just slow him down if I grabbed hold anywhere. I trotted along beside and watched.

An hour or so later we stood on the riverbank and
watched the current bear the corpse away.

"I can't tell you how happy this makes me," I
said.

"You just did," he said. "Let's head back."

We returned, but when he reached my place he
kept going.

"Where are we headed?" I finally asked, when he'd
turned left at the second crossroad.

"I'd said I went looking for you because I wanted
to speak with you. There is something I need to
show you first. If my timing is right, it's about midnight now."

"I'd guess it's close."

We approached the local church. There was a very
dim light from within.

"The front will probably be locked," he said. "We
wouldn't want to go in that way, though."

"We're going in?"

"That's my intention."

"Have you been in it before?"

"Yes. I know my way around. We'll go in the rear entrance if no one's about, pass through a small vestibule, turn left for a few paces, then right up a little hallway. We can get into the vestry from there, if it's clear."

"And then?"

"If we position ourselves properly, we get a view."

"Of what?"

"I'm curious myself. Let's find out."

We made our way around to the back of the building and listened. Determining that there was no one near on the other side, Larry rose up onto his hind legs, seeming far more graceful in that position than I could be. But then, he'd had a lot more practice. He seized the doorknob between his forepaws, squeezed, twisted, and pulled slowly.

It opened and we entered. He closed the door just as quietly behind us. We followed the route he had described, and, coming into the vestry, we were able to position ourselves to obtain the view he had referred to.

There was a service in progress.

Only a few people—one woman, the rest of them men—were present, occupying the front pews. The vicar stood before the altar—which I noted to be draped in black—and was reading to his congregation. He squinted through his square spectacles, as the flickering light was not very good, all of it coming from only a few black candles. Larry pointed out that the cross was upside-down, but I'd already noticed this myself.

"Do you know what that means?" he asked softly.

"Religious distress signal?" I said.

"Listen to what he's saying."

So I did.

" '. . . Nyarlathotep,' " he read, " 'cometh leaping upon the mountains, skipping upon the hills. He is like a many-legged goat, and he standeth behind our wall, he looketh forth at the windows, shewing himself through the lattice, horned in glory. Nyarlathotep spake, and he said, "Rise up, my dark one, and come away. For, lo, the winter is nigh and the cold rains fall. The flowers have died upon the earth, and the singing of birds is done. The turtle lies slain. The fig tree withers, as do the grapes. Arise, my dark one, and come away. . . ." ' "

The woman had risen to her feet, swaying slightly, and had begun to disrobe.

"You've proved your point," I said to Larry, memorizing the faces of the parishioners, whom I suspected to be the crossbow crew as well.

"Then let us take a hint and come away," he said.

I followed him from the vestry, and we let ourselves out the way we had come in. We made our way slowly back to the crossroads.

"So he's involved," I said after a time.

"It's *his* status I wanted to discuss with you."

"Yes?"

"I know that a certain geometry prevails in these matters, but I've never learned it fully," he said. "I do know, though, that it involves the placement of each player's residence."

"True. Oh. I see what you're getting at."

"Yes. How does his presence affect the pattern? Do you know how to figure these things, Snuff?"

"I do. I've been walking lines for some time. Where does he actually live?"

"That cottage behind the church is the vicarage."

"Okay. Close enough. I'm going to have to do a lot more calculating now."

"I need to know the center ground, the place of manifestation, Snuff."

"I'd guessed that, Larry, and I'll tell you when I figure it. Mind telling me your plans? I've a feeling they're special."

"Sorry."

"That makes you a part of my problem then, you know."

"How so?"

"If I don't know what you're up to, I don't know whether to count you as a player, whether or not to include your place in the diagram."

"I see."

He halted, there at the crossroads.

"Could you do it both ways—with me and without me—and let me know the results?"

"As well as both ways on the vicarage? That'd be damned complicated—having to work it both ways, twice. Why are you afraid to tell me? You've as much as said you're a closer. All right. So am I. You happy now? Your secret's safe. We're in this together."

"That's not it, Snuff," he said. "I can't tell you because I don't know. I'm an anticipator. I know certain things about the future, and I anticipate being at the center when the moon is full. And yes, I'm on your side. But I'll also be out of my mind that night. I still haven't worked out the formula for bringing it through a moon-change intact. I'm not sure I should even be categorized as a player. But then, I'm not sure I shouldn't. I'm just too much of a wild card."

I threw back my head and howled. Sometimes it's the best thing to do.

I went home, made my rounds, thought a lot, and slept. Earlier today, I encountered Graymalk as I paced the neighborhood and calculated.

"Hi, cat," I said.

"Hi, dog. What's the status on your disposal project?"

"Finished. Done. Complete. All floated away. Last night."

"Admirable. There were times when I thought they'd find it before you got there."

"Me, too."

"We have to be careful what we talk about now."

"Or even how we phrase things. But we're adults and we're reasonably intelligent and we both know the score. So, how's it going?"

"Not real well."

"Math problems?"

"I shouldn't say."

"It's all right. Everybody's got 'em just now."

"Do you know that? Or are you guessing?"

"It couldn't be any other way, believe me."

She stared at me.

"I do believe you. What I'd like to know is how you can be so sure?"

"That's the part I can't tell you, I'm afraid."

"I understand," she said. "But let's not stop talking just because we're into the second phase."

"Agreed. I think that would be a mistake."

"So, how's it going?"

"Not real well."

"Math problems or identity problems?"

"You're sharp. Both."

"If you solve the problem of whether Talbot's really a player, I'll trade you something for it."

"What?"

"Can't say, of course. But it could be useful if things get rough."

"I'm inclined to take you up on it, but I haven't an answer yet."

"That gives me something right there—small, but something. So, for whatever it's worth, here's a negative: It can't be the center of a road. The mistress has researched it and found good metaphysical reasons why not."

"I'd come to that conclusion myself, but I didn't know about the metaphysics. All right, we're still even."

"Talk to you again soon."

"Yes, soon."

I took a walk, to my favorite thinking place, a little hill to the northeast, whence I could see the entire area for a great distance. I called it Dog's Nest. I mounted the height of one of the big blocks of stone that lay there and was afforded a view of the township.

Identities. . . .

If neither Talbot nor the vicar were technically involved, I'd a good candidate for the center. And if only Larry were involved, it still held. Though I was leery of the Count, it would have to be checked out. But the vicar was also a wild card. If he were to be counted, but not Larry, an equally good candidate for center came into existence—one I had even visited recently. If he *and* Larry were both to be counted as players, though, a third possible site of manifestation was created, to the southeast—I hadn't quite figured where yet. I moved in a big circle about the hilltop, pissing on stone after stone as I calculated, partly to keep track of the lines, partly in frustration.

Then I had it, and I marked it in my mind. If they *both* played, then a big old manse about which I knew nothing was the third candidate for the locale. Excitement leaped in my breast like a puppy, enthusiastic and more than a little naive. A bit of consecration was all that was necessary to strengthen the probability of its choice. I'd have to check this out.

I realized then that I needed the help of a cat.

I went looking for Graymalk again but she was nowhere about. Cats are never around when you really need one. There was still time, though.

October 19

I WENT OUT LAST NIGHT AND SNIFFED around the ancient manse. There were signs of recent work on the place—smells of fresh-cut lumber, of paint, of roofing—but it was locked up tighter than a canopic urn, and I couldn't tell whether there was anyone about. I walked home, still feeling relieved that I was done with my corpse dragging. The wind whistled and dry leaves blew by me. There were flashes of lightning from off in the Good Doctor's direction.

The Thing in the Circle said, "French poodle?" when it saw me enter.

"Not today."

"Anything else? Anything at all? I'd sure like to get out and kill and rend. I'm feeling stronger all of a sudden."

"Your time will come," I told it.

The Thing in the Steamer Trunk had poked a small hole in the front. An enormous yellow eye regarded me through it. It didn't make a sound, though.

Snoring noises emerged from the wardrobe in the attic.

I paused before the mirror in the hall. All of its Things were clustered again, rather than slithering, and a close inspection showed me that they had positioned themselves before a small flaw in the glass which I hadn't noted earlier. Had they found a way to create such dimensional flaws in their prison? Still, it was too finite to be of much use to them. I resolved to keep an eye on it, though.

I awoke to the crunching sounds of wheels, the clopping of horses' hoofs, and the sounds of several voices, one of them singing in a foreign language, from the road out front. Stretching, and stopping for a quick drink of water, I let myself out to see what was going on.

It was a fine, crisp morning, of sunlight, breezes, and leaves crunching beneath my feet. A line of caravans was passing on the roadway, men in sashes and bright headcloths—Gipsies, all—walking beside or driving, headed, I guessed, for one of the open areas between us and the city, off in the direction of Larry Talbot's place.

"Good morning, Snuff," came a voice from the roadside weeds.

I walked over and investigated.

" 'Morning, Quicklime," I said, when I spotted his dark sinuosity there. "How you feeling?"

"Fine," he replied. "A lot better than the other day. Thanks for the advice."

"Any time. You headed anyplace in particular?"

"I was following the Gipsies, actually. But this is far enough. We'll get word where they camp, by and by."

"You think they'll be stopping near here?"

"Without a doubt. We've been expecting them for some time."

"Oh? Something special about them?"

"Well. . . . It's common knowledge now that the Count's in the area, so I'm not talking out of class. The master spent a lot of time in Eastern Europe, where he learned something of his ways. When the Count travels, he's often accompanied by a band of Gipsies. Rastov thinks he came here in a hurry when he determined where the locus would be, then sent for his band."

"What function will they serve here?"

"Now we're past the death of the moon, with the power rising, things get dangerous. Everybody seems to know where the Count's residing—unless he's established a few more, uh, residences. So someone with a fence picket who's decided the Game would be better off without him could end his eligibility. He likely wants his Gipsies about to guard his quarters by day—"

"Good Lords!" I said.

"What?"

"I hadn't even thought of the possibility of a player's having more than one residence. Do you realize what that would do to the pattern?"

"Damn! No, I hadn't! This is bad, Snuff. If he's got another grave or two somewhere that throws all the calculations off! It's good you thought of it, but what'll we do?"

"My first impulse was to keep it to myself," I said. "But then I realized we'll have to cooperate on this. We'll have to set up a schedule, take turns watching him come and go every night. If he's got another place—or places—we've got to find them."

"Maybe it would just be easier to stake the guy."

"That wouldn't solve the problem, though. It would just make it harder. And if he happens to be your ally—or mine? You could be sacrificing someone who'd make the difference."

"True. True. I wish I knew which side you were on. . . ."

"I'm not so sure that would be a good idea just yet. We may work together better for not knowing it."

" 'Work together. . . .' On the guard duty business, you mean?"

"I had a little more in mind, for us, right now, if you've got a little time."

"What do you have in mind?"

"I'll have to tell you a little of my calculations, but that's all right. Rastov has probably duplicated them by now—"

"*You* are the calculator in your pair?"

"That's right. Now, I propose telling you something, and then we'll go and check it out. No matter what we find, we'll learn something from it which will put us a little ahead."

"Of course I'll come."

"Good. My calculations show that one possible center of manifestation is that ruined church near where the Count is making his quarters. I don't know whether this is by accident or design. But either way it means that we can only check it by daylight. We'd better do it now, though, if there are going to be Gipsy guards around later."

"What exactly do you want to check?"

"I want you to slither down into the place and see whether it's suitable or whether there's not enough left for it to be our center. I'm too big to fit down the opening. I'll stand watch above and let you know if anyone comes by."

"I'll do it," he hissed. "Let's be on our way."

We started out.

"And you'll have to use your imagination, too. It may look bad, but if it could easily be enlarged by a few men with picks and shovels, tell me."

"Does this mean that Larry Talbot is a player?"

"It doesn't matter," I said. "It's one of the places it might be."

"What are the others?"

"Let's not get greedy," I said.

We made our way through the wood. When we reached the clearing there were no Gipsies about, nor anyone else.

"Check the crypt first," I said. "You've gotten me wondering whether he's still using it."

Quicklime slithered into its opening. A little later he returned.

"He's there," he reported, "and so's Needle. Both of them are asleep."

"Good. All right. Try the church now."

I paced about, sniffing the breezes, watching the trees. No one was near, no one approached.

In a little while Quicklime emerged.

"No," he said. "It's a complete disaster, filled with dirt and rocks. Nothing's left. We'd have to start over again and rebuild."

I approached the opening, forced myself in as far as I could. It narrowed quickly to the crack down which he had taken his way.

"How far back in that crack did you get?"

"Ten feet, maybe. There were two side ways off of it. Neither goes as far."

I believed him, from what I could see.

"So what does it mean?" he asked.

"That this isn't the place," I replied.

"Then what is?"

I thought quickly. I didn't like giving anything to the competition. But in this case one real fact could be misleading; and it was a fact he'd learn sooner or later, anyhow.

I backed out of the opening, turned toward the woods.

"Vicar Roberts," I said, "has a good disguise as a fanatic churchman. . . ."

"What do you mean?"

"He's a player."

"You're joking!"

"No. He holds midnight services to the Elder Gods, right there in the church."

"The vicar . . . ?"

"Check it out," I told him.

"What does that do to the pattern?"

"I've calculated that if we count the vicar and drop Larry Talbot that places the vicarage and the church at the center of the pattern. This isn't final if the Count is moving around, of course, but that's how it looks right now if we figure it this way."

"The vicar . . ." he repeated.

We entered the woods.

"So," he said after a while, "if the Count has a home away from home, or two, we need to find out whether they were established before or after the death of the moon."

"Yes," I agreed. Everything was frozen at that point. Death, relocation, withdrawal of a player—all of these shifted things about only before that time. Afterwards, we could kill each other or move about as we wished without disturbing the geometry of the business. "If there were a way of getting Needle to talk, we could find out."

"Hm," said Quicklime.

It occurred to me as we passed among the trees that I could be wrong, that I had just given him the correct information. But it seemed to me that the weight of Larry's presence—along with that anticipation business he spoke of—made him too big an influence on the game *not* to count him as a player, whether he collected ingredients and wove dueling spells, protections, opening spells, closing spells, or not. With him included—along with the vicar—it had to be that old manse rather than the church. And the oft-restored place looked as if it went back far enough to have a chapel around somewhere, or something that had once been a chapel.

Besides, it wasn't really a bad thing to reveal the vicar for what he was. The others would start doing things to skew his efforts once the word was out.

"So what about watching the Count's comings and goings?" I asked.

"Let's hold off on it, Snuff," he hissed. "No need to bring the others into this yet. I've a much better

idea for finding out about the Count's doings."

"Even with the Gipsies about?"

"Even so."

"What've you got in mind?"

"Let me pursue it on my own for a day or two. I promise I'll share it with you, after this. In fact, it would be a good idea. I think you're a better calculator than Rastov."

"All right. We'll hold off."

We parted at the edge of the wood, him going left, me right.

I made my way back to my place, did a quick circuit, found everything to be in order, and went back outside.

It was easy to follow the Gipsies' trail, since they stuck to the roadway till they neared their destination. It was a field near Larry's place. I lay doggo for an hour or two and watched them set up their encampment. I didn't really learn anything, but it was colorful.

Then I heard sounds from the road and turned my attention. An old-fashioned coach was approaching, drawn by two tired-looking horses. I dismissed it till it slowed and turned up Larry Talbot's driveway.

I quitted my place of concealment in a stand of shrubs and headed that way—in time to see the coachman help an old woman to descend from the vehicle. I moved nearer, passing among a few ancient trees, upwind of them, as the lady, with the assistance of a blackwood cane, made her way to Larry's front door. There, she raised the knocker and let it fall.

Shortly, Larry opened the door and they spoke

briefly. The wind prevented my making out their words, but after a short while he stepped aside and she entered.

Most peculiar. I circled the house to the rear, began peering in windows. I discovered them to be seated in the parlor, talking. Sometime later, Larry rose, absented himself briefly, returned with a tray bearing a decanter and a pair of glasses. He poured, and they sipped sherry, continuing their discussion. This went on for at least half an hour.

Finally, they both rose and departed the room. I raced about the house, checking windows again.

At last, I located them in the skylighted room where he grew his plants, engaged in an animated discussion with frequent gestures toward the flora. This went on for the better part of an hour, before they returned to the parlor for another glass of sherry and another long talk.

Then the coachman was summoned, and Larry loaded him with greenhouse clippings, then accompanied them both out to the coach before he bade her a cordial good-bye.

I was torn between following the coach and approaching Larry immediately. As the thing rumbled off, I realized that I could not contain myself—foolishly perhaps, for I can only speak with Jack between midnight and one o'clock. I raced up to him.

"Who was that lady?" I asked.

He smiled.

"Hello, Snuff. How are you?" he said.

I repeated my question, hoping that his canine spirit granted comprehension around the clock.

"A delightful lady," he replied. "Name's Linda Enderby. Widow of an India officer who'd died in the Mutiny. She and her servant recently moved into an old manse she's restored near here. The city's grown a bit dear for her, and far too busy. She was just paying a social call, wanting to meet some of the neighbors. And she shares my passion for botany. We had a lively discussion of dicotyledons."

"Oh," I said, ordering my thoughts. "I was watching the Gipsies when she arrived. I guess I assume everything involves the Game these days."

"Well, I guess they do, somehow," he said. "Gipsies and I go way back."

"I've heard the Count is sometimes associated with them."

"There's that, too," he said. "The whole matter will have to be explored, soon."

"I was concerned about your welfare," I said, truthfully.

"False alarm, Snuff," he said. "She's an intelligent and very personable lady. Would you care to come in? I have a beef stew you might—"

"No, thanks," I replied. "I've some errands I should be about. Thanks again for your help, the other night."

He smiled.

"No trouble, really. We'll talk again," he said, turning back toward his house.

"Yes."

I walked back slowly, thinking. I had caught their scents as I'd watched, and I knew Linda Enderby and her servant to be the Great Detective and his companion.

Leaves blew by, and I caught one in my teeth, spat it out again. The pace was quickening.

As I was approaching my home, there came a soft "Meow" from the field across the way.

"Gray?" I asked.

"Yes."

"Good. I wanted to talk to you."

"What a coincidence," she said.

I turned and entered the field. She was standing on the spot where the body had first been located.

"What about?" I asked her.

"I've decided not to play games with you. 'Ding, dong, dell,' as MacCab said."

"Oh. Well. . . ."

"What I thought you should know is that when the vicar was out with the searchers, this was the first place he brought them."

"Oh?"

"Yes. He had to know that the body was here. He wanted them to find it, wanted them to focus their investigation on Jack."

"How interesting."

". . . And how else would he know unless he'd left it here, or been party to it? Snuff, the vicar's behind it."

"Thank you."

"You're welcome."

I told her where the Gipsies were. She'd already seen them go by. So I told her, too, that we'd a new neighbor named Linda Enderby, who'd been by to visit Larry.

"Yes, I've met her," she said. "She was also by to visit

the mistress earlier. Charmed her completely. They share an interest in herbs and gourmet cooking."

"Jill's a gourmet cook?"

"Yes. Come by later, and I'll see that you get some choice selections."

"I'd like to do that. In fact, I'd like to collect you later, anyway. I want your help on an investigation."

"Of what?"

I had to tell her the truth if I wanted her help. So I told her of my conclusions on the hilltop, there in my ring of pissed-on stones, and of the day's adventures with Quicklime, of his speculations on the Gipsies, of the other things I'd learned about the vicar, and of my conclusions concerning the manse. I told her everything, except that the Great Detective had come to town and had set up housekeeping in that place, and that I could talk to Larry Talbot and get an answer anytime.

"I found a broken basement window when I was prowling the other night," I continued, "big enough for a cat to slip through easily."

". . . And you want me to go inside and see whether there's a chapel?"

"Yes."

"Of course I will. I have to know, too."

"When should I come by?"

"Just after dark."

I wandered for a little while after that, organizing my thoughts. My peregrinations took me past the church; a large albino raven regarding me, pink-eyed, from its peak. Circling the place once, for the sake of completeness, I saw the rotund coachman feeding his horses out back. Linda Enderby was paying a visit to the vicar.

October 20

I STOPPED BY GRAYMALK'S PLACE LAST NIGHT, per her invitation, and the mistress actually set down a plate of victuals for me on the back step. I realized then that Jill was far younger than I'd thought, now she wasn't wearing her Crazy clothes and had her hair down loose rather than tied back and hidden under a bandana. And she *was* a good cook. I can't remember when I'd eaten so well.

Afterwards, Graymalk and I headed for the manse. It was an exceptionally clear night, and there were stars all over the sky.

"It just occurred to me that you're a bird-watcher," I said.

"Of course."

"Have you seen an albino raven anywhere about?"

"As a matter of fact, I have, here and there, for several weeks now. Why?"

"It's occurred to me that it might be the vicar's

116

companion. Just a matter of proximity and a guess, really."

"I'll watch for it now, of course."

Someone with a crossbow passed us at a distance, moving in the other direction. We stood still, let him go by.

"Was that him?" she asked.

"Just a member of the midnight congregation," I said. "Not the man himself. Scent's wrong. I'll remember this one, though."

Streaks of high cirrus fluoresced above us from the stars they framed, and a gust of wind stirred my fur.

"I hunted rats and ate out of dustbins and saw my kittens killed and was hung by my tail and abused by wicked urchins," Graymalk said suddenly, "before the mistress found me. She was an orphan who'd lived on the streets. Her life had been even worse."

"Sorry," I said. "I've seen some bad times myself."

"If the way is opened, things should change."

"For the better?"

"Maybe. On the other paw, if it isn't opened, things may change, too."

"For the better?"

"Damned if I know, Snuff. Does anybody really care about a hungry cat, except for a few friends?"

"Maybe that's all anybody ever has, no matter how the big show is run."

"Still. . . ."

"Yes?"

"Hard times do really bring out the revolutionary in a person, don't they?"

"I'll give you that. Also, sometimes, the cynicism."

"Like you?"

"I suppose. The more things change. . . ."

"So that's the manse," she said suddenly, pausing to regard the big structure which had just come into view, a few lights visible within. "I've never been over this way before."

"No really unusual external features," I said, "and no—uh—dogs about. Let's go down and look around."

We did, making a circuit of the place, peering in windows, placing the Great Detective—one must give him credit for dedication to a role, as he was still in skirts—in the front parlor, reading, below a portrait of the Queen. His only lapse, if one might call it that, involved an occasional puff on a great calabash pipe which he rested between times in a rack on a table to his right. His companion lingered about the kitchen, preparing some small repast. There were many darkened rooms about the place. Off of the kitchen, we noted the head of a stairway leading downward.

"That's where I should be coming up," she said. "When I reach the top I'll pass through the kitchen, if he's gone by then, and explore the farther side of the house first. If he isn't, I'll go down the long hall on the near side and investigate all of its darkened chambers."

"Sounds like a good plan," I said.

We let ourselves down to ground level and rounded the corner to the basement window.

" 'Luck," I told her as she entered.

I went back to the window and watched the kitchen. The man was in no hurry to leave, nibbling as

he apparently waited for water to boil, taking out a
willow-pattern plate and bowl from a cupboard, nibbling some more, hunting out utensils from a drawer,
turning up from another cupboard one of those white
cups with the gold rim and gold flower inside that
everybody has, taking another nibble. . . . Finally, I
saw Graymalk at the head of the stair. How long she
had been there—unmoving, watching—I was uncertain. When his back was turned she slipped into the
near hall. As I had no vantage on that area, I made
a few circuits of the house to pass the time.

"Checking out our new neighbor, Snuff?" came a
voice from a tree to the east.

"It never hurts to be thorough," I replied. "What
about you, Nightwind?"

"The same. But she's not a player. We're almost
sure of it."

"Oh? You've met?"

"Yes. She visited the masters yesterday. They feel
she's harmless."

"Glad to know that someone is."

"Unlike the vicar, eh?"

"You've been talking to Quicklime."

"Yes."

"I thought you at odds. I heard you'd dropped him
in the river."

"A misunderstanding," he said. "We've smoothed
it over since."

"What did you give him for the vicar?"

"Needle's nightly feeding route," he said. "Maybe
he plans to ambush him and eat him." Nightwind
made a chuckling sound, something halfway between
hoot and gasp. "That would be amusing."

"Not to Needle."

He chuckled again.

"That's true, isn't it? I can almost hear him crying, 'This is not funny!' Then *gulp*, and we'd all have the last laugh."

"I've never eaten a bat," I said.

"They're not bad. A little salty, though. Say, since I've run into you maybe we can do a little business—nothing major, but we take whatever's there, eh?"

"Usually," I said. "What've you got?"

"After I heard about the vicar I went looking around his place. Met his companion—"

"A big white raven," I said. "I've seen it."

"Hm. Well, I decided on the direct approach. I flew up and introduced myself. Her name's Tekela, and she seemed behind on the Game and trying to catch up. Didn't have much to trade, but all she wanted was a list of the players and their companions. She'd get it from someone else if she didn't get it from me, I figured, and I might as well get whatever she had for it. First, though, she did know that you're one of us, and your bird-eating friend. She told me she'd seen you a few nights back, with another big dog, dragging a body toward the river. That was the missing officer, wasn't it?"

"I won't deny it."

"Did you or Jack kill him?"

"No. But the body turned up too near home for comfort."

"And you were just getting rid of it?"

"Would you want the thing in your front yard?"

"Certainly not. But what I'm curious about is your friend. Tekela recognized you as she swooped by, but

not the other dog. So she followed it when you parted. She said that it went to Larry Talbot's place."

"So?"

"We've been puzzled whether or not he's a player.
One argument against the assumption was that he
hadn't a companion. Now—"

"What was Tekela doing way in the hell out in
that field that night?" I asked.

"Presumably, she was patrolling the area in general,
as we all do."

" 'Presumably'?" I said. "Her master was involved
in that man's death, and she went looking for the
body after I'd moved it and found it. She was keeping
an eye on it to see whether whoever'd put it there
would be back to do any more with it."

He was silent, and he shrank a little within his
feathers. Then, "That's what I was going to trade you
for the story on Larry's companion," he said. "But do
you know *how* he died? She did tell me that."

Just then I saw it. I'd a vision of the officer, drugged,
knocked out, or tied up upon the altar as the vicar
blessed an edged instrument.

"Ceremonial killing," I said, "at one of his midnight services. It was early in the cycle for one. But
that's what happened. Then he left the remains at
our place for a bit of misdirection."

"He needed it early for the extra power, because
he'd gotten off to a late start. All right. I'll give you
something else for Talbot."

"Concerning what?"

"The Good Doctor."

"Done. I haven't heard anything about him for a
while. The dog is a stray from town. Name's Lucky.

I give him some of my food when he's around and he does favors for me. He hangs around Talbot's place, too, because Talbot saves scraps for him. He's too big for anyone to want to feed on a regular basis, though, which is why he hasn't a real home. You might even spot him in the woods or fields some night, hunting rabbits."

"Oh," Nightwind said, rotating his head ninety degrees to stare at the manse. "That spoils one of Morris's new theories. You're a calculator, aren't you?"

"My, Quicklime was chatty."

"It just came out in passing," he said. "If Talbot were indeed a player, and with the vicar now in the Game . . . well, things would be moved around interestingly, wouldn't they?"

"Yes," I admitted.

"So we're both checking the place out."

"True," I said. "I don't *know* that Talbot's not a player. But if he is, Lucky's not his companion."

"Interesting. Have you—or Lucky—seen any other candidates about his place?"

"No. He seems to prefer plants to animals."

"Can a plant be a companion?"

"I don't know. They're alive, but kind of limited in what they can do. I don't know. Maybe."

"Well, this will all shake down in a few days, I'm sure. In ample time for the work to be done and the world—Should I say 'redeemed' or 'preserved'?"

"Let us say 'messed with,' either way."

He closed his left eye and opened it again.

"And the Good Doctor?" I prompted.

"Ah, yes," he replied. "He was the other one Tekela knew about. But I was intrigued when she

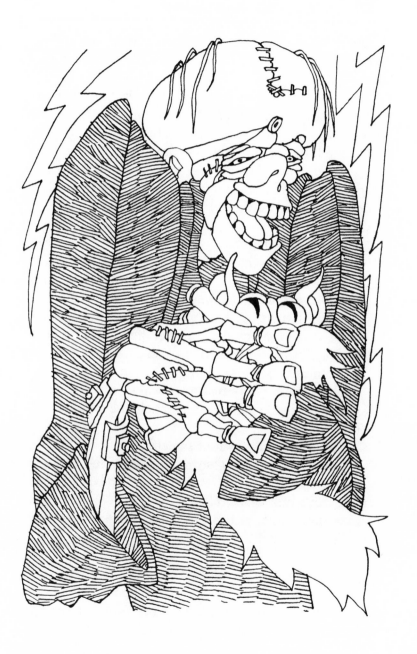

insisted that there are three people living out there, not two."

"Oh?"

"So I flew out to investigate, during another of those nasty storms that always seem in progress in the area. And she was right. There was a big fellow lurching about the place—drunk perhaps. Biggest man I've ever seen. He was only about for a little while, during the height of the storm. Then he lay down on that fancy bed in the basement, and the Good Doctor covered him up, entirely, with a sheet. He didn't stir again."

"Strange. Bubo have anything to say about this?"

"Bah! You ought to send Graymalk after him, if I don't get him first. Rats aren't as salty as bats. Tougher, though. . . . He's worthless for information. Won't trade for anything. Either he's stupid, ignorant, or just closemouthed."

"I don't think he's stupid."

"Then I'm not sure he knows where his best interests lie. Either way, he's not much use to the rest of us."

"I'll have to corner him sometime."

"Don't eat the tail. They're no good." He chuckled again. "If you find out more about Talbot or this place, let's talk again. Plants . . . hm?"

He spread his wings and swooped away to the south. I watched him vanish into the night. Formidable.

I circled the manse again, checking at a few windows. Then I heard the back door open. I was near the front at the time, and I rushed around, concealing myself behind a tree.

"Good kitty," said the Great Detective, in a well-controlled falsetto, "come visit us again sometime."

Graymalk was deposited on the back steps and the door was closed. I cleared my throat, but she sat there for a time grooming herself before wandering off in the other direction. Suddenly, she was beside me.

"Are you all right?" I asked her.

"Fine," she said. "Let's walk."

I headed southward.

"She has a good memory, that old lady," Gray finally said.

"In what respect?"

"Her servant spotted me, on a sudden return to the kitchen, and she heard me call out. She came back and called me by name. She was very nice. Even gave me a saucer of milk, which I felt obliged to drink. Who'd've thought anyone would look at a cat well enough to recognize her later—not to mention remembering her name?"

"Maybe she likes cats. Must have, if she wanted to feed you."

"In that case, you'd think she'd have one of her own. But she doesn't. There were no signs."

"Just has a good eye and a good memory then, I guess."

We crossed the road, kept going.

"I guess so," she said. "So, I got to look around pretty well before they found me."

"And . . . ?"

"There's a windowless room with a wide door and a niche in its far wall—which is of stone, by the way. That old place has been through a lot of changes. Anyway, the niche seemed about right to have held an altar at one time. There were even a few small crosses chiseled into the stone, and a bit of Latin—I think it was."

"Good," I said, "in one way."

"What's the other way?"

"Nightwind knows about it. He came by while you were inside, and we talked. The white raven, by the way, is named Tekela."

"Oh, he knows her?"

". . . And you were right about the vicar. It was a ceremonial killing—dues for getting into the Game late."

"Sounds as if you had a long talk."

"We did. I'd better fill you in."

"Any special reason we're heading this way?"

"Yes. That's part of it."

We continued to the south and a bit to the west as I told her the things I'd learned. The air grew moist as we went and the sky dark as a blot in that particular area about which heaven's artillery flickered and boomed.

"So you want to peer in the Good Doctor's windows again?"

"In a word, yes."

"Cats aren't real fond of getting wet," she observed, after the soft weather got harder.

"Dogs aren't crazy about it either," I said. Then, "Whoever wins, it'll still rain."

She made the closest sound I'd ever heard her manage to a laugh—a little rhythmic, musical thing.

"That's true," she said a little later, "I'm sure. How many times in a century does the Full Moon rise on Halloween—three, four?"

"It varies," I responded. "It's more interesting to ask, on how many of those occasions do the appropriate people assemble to try for an opening or hold for a closing?"

"I couldn't guess. This is your first, of course."

"No," I said, and I did not elaborate, knowing what I had just given away.

We walked on through the drizzle toward the place of brightnesses, keeping to the road as there were fewer wet things to brush up against there.

As we drew nearer, I saw that the front door of the farmhouse stood open, light spilling out through its rectangle. And someone was moving upon the roadway, headed toward us. Another discharge from the storm clouds gave the building a thorny corona of light, and outlined briefly in its glare I saw that a very big man was moving toward us at an ungainly but extremely rapid pace. He was dressed in ill-fitting garments, and my single glimpse of his face showed it as somehow misshapen, lopsided. He halted before us, swaying, turning his head from side to side. Fascinated, I stared. The rain had washed all scents from the air, until we achieved this proximity. Now, though, I could smell him and he grew even stranger to me, for it was the sick, sweet scent of death that informed his person, reached outward from it. His movements were not aggressive, and he regarded us with something akin to a child's simple curiosity.

A tall figure suddenly appeared at the farmhouse door, looking outward into the night, laboratory coat flapping in the wind.

The giant figure before me leaned forward, staring into my face. Slowly, unthreateningly, he extended his right hand toward me and touched me on the head.

"Good—dog," he said in a harsh, cracked voice, "good—dog," as he patted me.

Then he turned his attention to Graymalk, and moving with a speed that belied his earlier gesture, he snatched her up from the ground and held her to his breast.

"Kit-ty," he said then. "Pret-ty kit-ty."

Clumsily, he moved to stroke her with his other hand, rain streaming down his face now, dripping from his garments.

"Pret-ty—"

"Snuff!" Graymalk wailed. "He's hurting me! Too tight! His grip's too tight!"

I began barking immediately, hoping to distract him into relaxing his grip.

"Hello!" came a call from the man at the farmhouse. "Come back! You must come back now!"

I kept barking, and the man dashed outside, rushing in our direction.

"He's let up a little, but I still can't get free!" Graymalk told me.

Apparently confused, the huge man turned to the approaching figure, and back again. It appeared to be the Good Doctor headed our way. I kept up the barking, since it seemed to have worked.

When the Good Doctor came up beside the giant he placed a hand upon his arm.

"Raining cats and dogs, I see," he said.

I stopped barking as the giant turned his head and stared at him, doubtless at a loss for words in the face of such a sallying of wit.

"The doggy wants you to put the kitty down," he told him. "The kitty wants to get down, too. Put her down and come back with me now. It's a bad night to be outside—with all this rain."

"Bad—night," the big man responded.

"Yes. So put the kitty down and come with me."

"Bad—rain," rejoined the other.

"Indeed. Cat. Down. Now. Come. Now. With me."

"Cat—kitty—down," said the big fellow, and he leaned forward and deposited Graymalk gently on the road. His eyes met mine as he rose, and he added, "Good—dog."

"I'm sure," said the Good Doctor, taking hold of his arm with both hands now and turning him back toward the farmhouse.

"Let's get out of here," Graymalk said, and we did.

October 21

THE THINGS ARE GETTING RESTLESS, BUT their restraints still serve. I stopped by Larry's place this morning, to suggest he answer to the name "Lucky," if so addressed by any woodsy denizen in his wanderings. This necessitated my giving him a little background concerning speculations as to his status. He's agreed to be even more circumspect in his comings and goings. I filled him in on all the rest, too, since I considered us partners. Everything, that is, save for Linda Enderby's true identity. I was loath to destroy his illusions concerning the genial old lady whose company had given him such pleasure. Whatever had been learned there had been learned—and I doubted it could have been much in such a bizarre case as his, with him so guarded concerning it—and letting him live a little longer with his fond memory of the visit did not seem much in the way of risk taking. I resolved to wait a few days before revealing the deception.

"Hear anything more about the police and their search?" I asked.

"They're still investigating, but they seem to have questioned everyone and now they've started searching fields along the way. I think the latest theory is that the officer might have been thrown from his horse—which did make it back to their stables."

"I guess he didn't wash up. Maybe he made it out to sea."

"Possibly. I'm sure they'd be looking at any washups pretty closely."

"I wonder what this beating of the bushes might mean to the Count, if they go very far afield?"

"I'll bet if you check today you'll find he's moved."

"So you think he has another place, too?"

"Of course. That's his style. And he has the right idea. Everyone should have a place to run to. You can never be too careful."

"Do you?"

He smiled.

"I hope you do, too," he said.

When I smile no one can tell.

I went looking for Graymalk then, to see whether I could persuade her to climb down into the crypt for me again. But she wasn't anywhere about. Finally, I gave up and wandered over to Rastov's place.

Quicklime wasn't readily available either, and I began rearing up and peering in windows. I spotted Rastov himself, slouched in a chair, vodka bottle in one hand, what might be his icon clutched to his breast with the other. Something stirred on the windowsill and I realized it to be my erstwhile partner. Quicklime

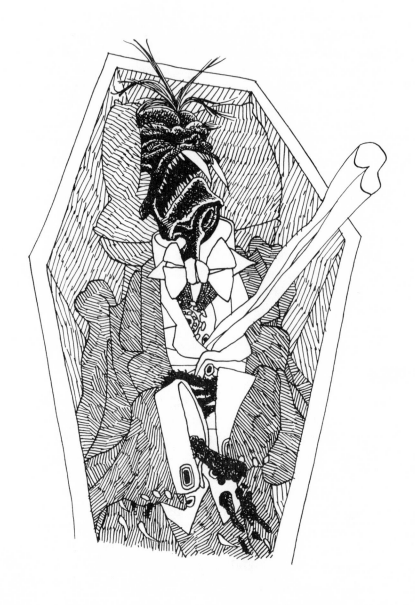

raised his head, stared at me, then gestured with his head toward the adjacent room. At that, he slid from the sill and was gone.

I made my way back to the near window of that room, which was opened slightly. Moments later, he emerged.

"Hi, Quick," I said. "How's it going?"

"Sometimes I wish I were back in the fields again," he replied. "I'd be getting ready for a long winter's sleep."

"Bad night?"

"I got out just in time. He's at it again. Drinking and singing sad songs. He could get us into a lot of trouble when he's had too much. He'd better be sober for the big night."

"I should hope so."

We went off toward the rear of the place.

"Busy?" he asked me.

"Believe it."

"Listen, Snuff, the boss doesn't tell me everything, and Nightwind said—just a day or two back—that there are divinatory ways for discovering whether someone's an opener or a closer. Is that true?"

"He's right," I said. "But they're unreliable before the death of the moon. You really have to have some juice to make them work."

"How soon after?"

"Several days."

"So people could be finding out everyone's status pretty soon?"

"Yes, they will. They always do. That's why it's important to finish any mutual business before then. Once the lines are drawn, your former partners may be your new enemies."

"I don't like the idea of having you or Nightwind for an enemy."

"It doesn't follow that we have to kill each other before the big event. In fact, I've always looked on such undertakings as a sign of weakness."

"But there's always *some* killing."

"So I've heard. Seems a waste of energy, though, when such things will be taken care of at the end, anyhow."

". . . And half of us will die in the backlash from the other half's winning."

"It's seldom a fifty-fifty split of openers and closers. You never know what the disposition will be, or who will finally show up. I heard there was once an attempt where everyone withdrew on the last day. Nobody showed. Which was wrong, too. Think of it. Any one of them with guts enough could have had it his own way."

"How soon till the word gets out, Snuff?"

"Pretty soon. I suppose someone could be working on it right now."

"Do *you* know?"

"No. I'll know soon enough. I don't like knowing till I have to."

He crawled up onto an old tree stump. I sat down on the ground beside him.

"For one thing," I said, "it would interfere in my asking you to do something just now."

"What," he said, "is it?"

"I want you to come back with me to the crypt and check it out. I want to know whether the Count's still there."

He was silent, turning in the sunlight, scales shimmering.

"No," he said then. "We don't have to go."

"Why not?"

"I already know that he's not there."

"How do you know this?"

"I was out last night," he said, "and I hung myself in a plum tree I'd learned Needle frequents when he feeds. When he came by I said, 'Good evening, Needle.'

" 'Quicklime, is that you?' he answered.

" 'Indeed,' I replied, 'and how go your farings?'

" 'Well. Well,' he said. 'And your own twisting ways?'

" 'Oh, capital,' I answered. 'I take it you have come to feed?'

" 'Yes. I always come here last, for these plums are my favorites and put a fine end to a harvesting of bugs. I prefer saving the best for last.'

" 'As it should be,' I said, 'with all endeavors. Tell me'—for I was wise in these ways now, having lived with Rastov—'have you ever sampled the long-fallen plums, those which look wrinkled, ruined, and unappetizing?'

" 'No,' he replied, 'that would be silly, when so many good ones still hang upon the tree.'

" 'Ah,' I told him, 'but looks may be deceptive, and "good" is certainly a relative term.'

" 'What do you mean?' he asked.

" 'I, too, enjoy the fruits,' I said, 'and I have learned their secret. Those over yonder on the ground are far better than those which hang yet upon the limbs.'

" 'How can that be?' he said.

" 'The secret is that as they lie there, cut off forever from the source of their existence, they draw upon their remaining life to continue a new kind of growth. True, the effects wither them, but they ferment from their own beings a new and special elixir, superior to the simple juices of those upon the tree.'

" 'They taste a lot better?'

" 'No. They do not. This goes beyond mere taste. It is a thing of the spirit.'

" 'I guess I ought to try it, then.'

" 'You will not be disappointed. I recommend it highly.'

"So he descended to the earth, came upon one of those I had indicated, and bit into it.

" 'Agh!' he exclaimed. 'These are no good! Overripe and—'

" 'Give it a chance,' I said. 'Take more, swallow it down, and then some more. Wait just a bit.'

"And he sampled again, and again.

"A little later, he said, 'I feel slightly dizzy. But it is not unpleasant. In fact—'

"He tried another, suddenly more enthusiastic. Then another.

" 'Quicklime, you were right,' he said after a while. 'There is something very special about them. There is a warm feeling—'

" 'Yes,' I answered.

" 'And the dizziness is not quite dizziness. It feels good.'

" 'Take more. Take lots more,' I told him. 'Go with it as far as it will take you.'

"Shortly, his words grew harder to understand, so that I had to slide down from the tree to be sure I heard everything he said when I began, 'You were with the Count when he created his new graves, were you not . . . ?'

"And so I learned their locations, and that he was moving to one last night," he finished.

"Well done," I said. "Well done."

"I hope he didn't awaken feeling the way I did the other morning. I did not linger, for I gather it is a bad thing to see snakes when you are in that condition. At least, Rastov says it is. With me, it was humans that I saw last time—all those passing Gipsies. Then yourself, of course."

"How many graves are there besides the crypt?"

"Two," he said. "One to the southwest, the other to the southeast."

"I want to see them."

"I'll take you. The one to the southwest is nearer. Let's go there first."

We set out, crossing a stretch of countryside I had not visited before. Eventually, we came to a small graveyard, a rusted iron fence about it. The gate was not secured, and I shouldered it open.

"This way," Quicklime said, and I followed him.

He led me to a small mausoleum beside a bare willow tree.

"In there," he said. "The vault to the right is opened. There is a new casket within."

"Is the Count inside it?"

"He shouldn't be. Needle said he'd be sleeping at the other one."

I entered nevertheless and pawed at the lid for some while before I found a way to open it. When I did, it came up quite easily. It was empty, except for a handful or two of dirt at its bottom.

"It looks like the real thing," I said. "Take me to the other one now."

We set off on the longer trek, and as we went I asked, "Did Needle tell you when these graves were established?"

"Several weeks ago," he answered.

"Before the dark of the moon?"

"Yes. He was very insistent on the point."

"This will ruin my pattern," I said, "and everything seemed such a perfect fit."

"Sorry."

"You're sure that's what he said?"

"Positive."

"Damn."

The sun shone brightly, though there were clouds about—and, of course, a goodly cluster off toward the Good Doctor's place, farther south—and there came a bit of chill with a northerly breeze. We made our way cross-country through the colors of autumn—browns, reds, yellows—and the ground was damp, though not spongy. I inhaled the odors of forest and earth. Smoke curled from a single chimney in the distance, and I thought about the Elder Gods and wondered at how they might change things if the way were opened for their return. The world could be a good place or a nasty place without supernatural intervention; we had worked out our own ways of doing things, defined our own goods and evils. Some gods were great for individual ideals to be aimed at, rather than actual ends to be sought, here and now. As for the Elders, I could see no profit in intercourse with those who transcend utterly. I like to keep all such things in abstract, Platonic realms and not have to concern myself with physical presences. . . . I breathed the smells of woodsmoke, loam, and rotting windfall apples, still morning-rimed, perhaps, in orchard's shade, and saw a high, calling flock V-ing its way to the south. I heard a mole, burrowing beneath my feet. . . .

"Does Rastov drink like that every day?" I asked.

"No," Quicklime replied. "He only started on Moondeath Eve."

"Has Linda Enderby visited him?"

"Yes. They had a long talk about poetry and someone named Pushkin."

"Do you know whether she got a look at the Alhazred Icon?"

"So you know we have it. . . . No, drunk or sober, he wouldn't show it to anybody till the time of its need."

"When I was looking for you earlier, I saw him holding what looked like an icon. Is it on wood, about three inches high, nine inches long?"

"Yes, and he did have it out from its hiding place today. Whenever he feels particularly depressed he says that it cheers him up to 'go to the shores of Hali and consider the enactments of ruin' and then to contemplate the uses he has for it all."

"That could almost be taken as a closer's statement," I said.

"I sometimes think you're a closer, Snuff."

Our eyes met, and I halted. At some point, you have to take a chance.

"I am," I said.

"Damn! We're not alone then!"

"Let's keep it quiet," I said. "In fact, let's not speak of it again."

"But you can at least tell me whether you know if any of the others are."

"I don't," I said.

I started forward again. A small plunge taken, a small victory grasped. We passed a pair of cows, heads down, munching. A small roll of thunder came from the Good Doctor's direction. Looking left, I could make out my hill, which I'd named Dog's Nest.

"Is this one farther south than the other?" I asked, as we turned onto a lane which led in that direction.

"Yes," he hissed.

I kept trying to visualize the pattern tugged in new directions by these new foci of residence. It was irritating to keep finding and losing candidates for center. It seemed almost as if the forces were playing games with me. And it was especially difficult to keep surrendering ones that seemed eminently appropriate.

At last our way took us to what seemed like somebody's family plot. Only, the family it belonged to was long gone. A collapsed building lay upon a nearby hilltop. Barely a foundation, really, was what remained. And I saw that the remains of the family had been adopted, when Quicklime led me into the overgrown graveyard, all but the eastern side of its fence fallen, and that side atilt.

He led me among tall grasses to a great stone slab. There were signs of recent digging about the perimeter it had covered, and the stone had been raised and offset to the side, leaving a narrow opening through which I knew I must squeeze.

I stuck my nose inside and sniffed. Dust.

"Want me to check it out?" Quicklime said.

"Let's both go down," I replied. "After this walk, I at least want a look."

I went through and descended a series of uneven steps. There was a puddle at the bottom and I stepped over it. There were others about, too, and I couldn't avoid them all. It was dark, but eventually I made out an opened casket set up in a raised area. Another had been moved aside to make room for it.

I approached to sniff about the thing. What odors I might have sought, I'm not sure. The Count had been scentless on the night we had met, a very disconcerting thing to one of my temperament and olfactory equipment. As I drew nearer and my vision cleared, I wondered why he had left the lid open. It seemed most inappropriate for one of his persuasion.

Rearing up, I placed a forepaw on the casket's side and looked down into the interior.

Quicklime, nearby, said, "What is it?" and I realized that I had made a small woofing sound.

"The Game has grown more serious," I answered.

He climbed up to the ledge, then mounted the end of the casket where he hovered, looking like Pharaoh's headdress.

"Oh my!" he said then.

A skeleton lay within, atop a long black cloak. It still had on a suit of dark garments, somewhat in disarray now, opened in front. Splitting the sternum was a large wooden stake, angled slightly, passing far down, missing the backbone to the left. There was considerable dry dust within and without.

"Looks like the new site wasn't as secret as he'd thought," I said.

"Wonder whether he was an opener or a closer?" Quicklime said.

"I'd've guessed 'opener,' " I said, "but I suppose we'll never know."

"Who do you think nailed him?"

"I've no idea, yet," I said, lowering myself and turning away. I squinted into nooks and fissures then. "See Needle anywhere about?" I asked.

"No. You think they got him, too?"

"Could be. If he turns up, though, he'll certainly bear questioning."

I climbed the stair and emerged into light. I started walking back.

"What happens now?" Quicklime asked.

"I have to make my rounds," I said.

"Do we just go on and wait for it to happen again?"

"No. We exercise caution."

We slithered and trotted back to our own area.

Jack was out, and I took care of business about the house and went looking for Graymalk to fill her in on the latest. Was surprised to encounter Jack engaged in conversation with Crazy Jill on her back step. He had in his hand a cup of sugar which he had presumably just borrowed. He ended the conversation and turned away as I approached. Graymalk was nowhere about. Jack told me as I walked him home that we might ride into town for supplies of a mundane nature sometime soon.

Later, I was out front, still looking for Graymalk, when the Great Detective's coach passed, him still in his Linda Enderby guise. Our eyes met and held for several long seconds. Then he was gone.

I went back inside and took a long nap.

I awoke near dusk and made the rounds again. The Things in the Mirror were still clustered, and pulsing lightly. The flaw appeared slightly larger, though this could have been a trick of memory and imagination. I resolved to call it to Jack's attention soon, however.

Eating and drinking and passing outside then, I sought Graymalk once more. I found her in her front yard doing catnappery on the steps.

"Hello. Looked for you earlier," I said. "Missed you."

She yawned and stretched, cleaned her shoulders.

"I was out," she responded, "checking around the church and the vicarage."

"Did you get inside?"

"No. Looked into every opening I could, though."

"Learn anything interesting?"

"The vicar keeps a skull on the desk in his study."

"*Memento mori*," I remarked. "Churchmen are some-times big on that sort of thing. Maybe it came with the place as a part of the furnishings."

"It's resting in the bowl."

"The bowl?"

"*The* bowl. The old pentacle bowl they talk about."

"Oh." So I'd been wrong in assigning that tool to the Good Doctor. "That accounts for an item." Then, disingenuously, "Now, if you can tell me where the two wands are . . ." I said.

She gave me a strange look and continued grooming herself.

". . . And I had to climb the outside of the place," she said.

"Why?"

"I heard someone crying upstairs. So I made my way up the siding and looked in what seemed the proper window. I saw a girl on a bed. She had on a blue dress, and there was a long chain around her ankle. The other end was attached to the bed frame."

"Who was it?"

"Well, I met Tekela a little later," she went on. "I don't think she was too eager to talk to a cat. Still, I persuaded her to tell me that the girl is Lynette, the daughter of the vicar's late wife Janet by a previous marriage."

"Why was she chained up?"

"Tekela said that she was being disciplined for attempting to run away."

"Very suspicious. How old is she?"

"Thirteen."

"Yes. Just right. Sacrifice, of course."

"Of course."

"What did you give her for the information?"

"I told her the story of our encounter with the big man the other night—and the possibility that the Gipsies may be associated with the Count."

"I'd better tell you something about the Count," I said, and I detailed my investigations with Quicklime.

"No matter whose side he was on, I can't say I'm sorry to see him out of the picture," she said. "He was extremely frightening."

"You met him?"

"I saw him one night, departing that first crypt. I'd hidden myself on a tree limb, to watch it happen. He seemed to ooze up out of there as if he weren't really moving any muscles, just flowing, the way Quicklime can do. Then he stood there a moment with his cloak flapping about him in the wind, turning his head, looking at the world as if he owned it and was deciding what part of it would amuse him just then. And then he laughed. I'll never forget that sound. He just threw his head back and barked—not the way you do, unless you've a special way of barking just before you eat something that might not want to be eaten, and that this pleases you, adds to the flavor. Then he moved, and it played tricks with my eyes. He was different things, different shapes, flapping cloak all about—even in different places at the same time—and then he was gone, like a piece of the cloak sailing away in the moonlight. I wasn't unhappy to see him go."

"I never saw anything that dramatic," I said. "But I met him at even closer quarters, and I was impressed." I paused, then, "Did Tekela give you anything besides the story on Lynette?" I asked.

"Everyone seems to be onto the idea of the old manse as the center now," she said. "The vicar told her that it had served a much larger church, south of here, in the old days—one that the last Henry had ruined, as an example to the others that he meant business."

"That makes it such a good candidate that I'm irritated at the Count's bad taste in throwing off the calculations."

"Have you figured the new site yet?"

"No. I should be about that pretty soon, though."

"You'll let me know?"

"I'll take you with me when I do it," I offered.

"When will that be?"

"Probably tomorrow. I was just going to walk up the road to see the Gipsies now."

"Why?"

"They're sometimes colorful. You can come along if you like."

"I will."

We headed on up the road. It was another clear-skied night, with multitudes of stars. I could hear a distant music as we neared Larry's place. Beyond, I could make out the glow of bonfires. As we continued, I could distinguish the sounds of violin, guitar, tambourine, and a single drum within the music. We drew nearer, coming at last to a hiding place beneath a caravan, from which we could watch. I smelled dogs, but we were downwind and none bothered us.

Several older Gipsy women were dancing and there was suddenly a singer making wailing sounds. The music was stirring, the dancers' movements stylized, like the steps of long-legged birds I'd seen in warmer climes. There were many fires, and from some of them came the smells of cooking. The spectacle was as much a thing of the shadows as the light, however, and I rather liked the wailing, being something of a connoisseur when it comes to barks and howls. We watched for some time, taken by the bright colors of the dancers' and players' garments as much as by the movements and the sounds.

They played several tunes, and then the fiddler gestured toward a knot of spectators, holding out his instrument and pointing to it. I heard a sound of protest, but he insisted, and finally a woman moved forward into the light. It was several moments before I realized it to be Linda Enderby. Obviously, the Great

Detective was making yet another of his social calls. Back in the shadows, I could now make out the short, husky form of his companion.

Over several protests, he accepted the violin and bow, touched the strings, then cradled the instrument as if he knew its kind well. He raised the bow, paused for a long moment, and then began to play.

He was good. It was not Gipsy music, but was some old folk tune I'd heard somewhere before. When it was done he moved immediately into another on which he worked several variations. He played and he played, and it grew wilder and wilder—

Abruptly, he halted and took a step, as if suddenly moving out of a dream. He bowed then and returned the instrument to its owner, his movements in that moment entirely masculine. I thought of all the controlled thinking, the masterfully developed deductions, which had served to bring him here, and then this— this momentary slipping into the wildness he must keep carefully restrained—and then seeing him come out of it, smiling, becoming the woman again. I saw in this the action of an enormous will, and suddenly I knew him much better than as the pursuing figure of many faces. Suddenly I knew that he had to be learning, as we were learning other aspects, of the scope of our enterprise, that he could well be right behind us at the end, that he was almost, in some way, a player—more a force, really—in the Game, and I respected him as I have few beings of the many I have known.

Later, as we walked back, Graymalk said, "It was good to get away for a time."

"Yes," I said, "it was," and I regarded the sky, where the moon was growing.

October 22

"A CHIHUAHUA?" THE THING IN THE CIRCLE suggested. "Just for laughs?"

"Nope," I answered. "Language barrier."

"Come on!" it said. "I'm almost strong enough to break out of here on my own now. It won't go well with you if you keep me till I do."

" 'Almost,' " I said, "isn't good enough."

It growled. I growled back. It flinched. I was still in control.

The Thing in the Steamer Trunk had become a lot more active, too, glaring at me through its aperture. And we had to install a sliding bar on the wardrobe in the attic, as the Thing there succeeded in breaking the latch. But I drove it back again. I was still in control there, too.

I went outside then, checking for foci of interference. Finding nothing untoward, I walked over to Larry's place, intending to bring him up to date on everything and to see what news he might have. I halted as it came into sight, though. The Enderby coach was parked out front, the heavy man beside it. Had I let this go on too long? What might the Great Detective find so fascinating here that it warranted a return visit? Nothing I could do now, of course.

I turned and walked back.

When I reached the neighborhood I found Graymalk waiting in my yard.

"Snuff," she said, "have you been calculating?"

"Only in my head," I replied. "I think it might be easier to work this one out from a vantage."

"What vantage?"

"Dog's Nest," I said. "If you're interested, come on."

She fell into step beside me. The air was damp, the sky gray. A wind gusted out of the northeast.

We passed Owen's place and Cheeter chattered at us from a branch:

"Odd couple! Odd couple!" he called. "Opener, closer! Opener, closer!"

We did not respond. Let the divinators have their day.

"It is an odd curse you are under," Graymalk remarked after a long while.

"Say rather that we are the keepers of a curse. Perhaps more than one. If you live long enough, these things have a way of accumulating. How do you know of it?"

"Jack said something of it to the mistress."

"How strange. It is not usually a thing we speak of."

"There must be a reason."

"Of course."

"So you have been present at more than one. You have played the Game—many times?"

"Yes."

"Do you think he might be trying to persuade her to change—orientation?"

"Yes."

"I wonder what it would be like?"

We passed Rastov's place but did not stop. On the road, later, MacCab went by, a stick in his hand. He raised it as we neared, and I snarled at him. He lowered it and muttered a curse. I am used to curses, and no one can tell when I smile.

We continued into the countryside, coming at length to my hill. There we climbed to the place of fallen and standing stones. Southward of us, the black clouds rumbled and glared above the Good Doctor's house.

The winds were stronger at this height, and as I paced the circle a small rain began to descend. Graymalk crouched on the dry side of a block of stone, watching me as I took my sightings.

Out of the southwest, I took my line from the distant graveyard, extending it to all of the other points of residence in view or in mind. Then, from the place where lay the Count's remains, I did it again. In my mind, I beheld the new design. This pulled the center away from the manse, downward, southward, passing us, coming to rest ahead, slightly to the left. I stood stock-still, the rain forgotten, as I worked it out, repeating the process line by line, seeing that center shift, positing where it had to fall. . . .

Again, the same area. But there was nothing there, no outstanding feature. Just a hillside, a few trees and rocks upon it. No structures at all nearby.

"Something's wrong," I muttered.

"What is it?" Graymalk said.

"I don't know. It's just not right. In the past, they've always at least been interesting, acceptable candidates. But this is—nothing. Just a dull stretch of field to the south and a little to the west."

"All of the other candidates have also been wrong," she said, coming over, "no matter how interesting." She mounted a nearby stone. "Where is it?"

"Over there," I said, pointing with my head. "To the right of those five or six trees clustered on that hillside."

She stared.

"You're right," she said. "It doesn't look particularly promising. You sure you calculated correctly?"

"Double-checked," I answered.

She returned to her shelter again, as the rain suddenly grew more forceful. I followed her.

"I suppose we must visit it," she said a little later. "After this lets up, of course."

She began licking herself. She hesitated.

"I just thought of something," she said. "The Count's skeleton. Was that big ring he wore still upon his finger?"

"No," I said. "Whoever did him in doubtless collected it."

"Then someone's probably doubly endowed."

"Probably."

"That would make him stronger, wouldn't it?"

"Only in technical prowess. It might make him more vulnerable, too."

"Well, the technical end of things counts for something."

"It does."

"Do the Games always get confusing at some point? Do they mess up the players' thinking, ideas, values?"

"Always. Especially as events begin to cascade and accelerate near the end. We create a kind of vortex about us just by being here and doing certain things. Your confusion may trip you up. Somebody else's confusion may save you."

"You're saying that it gets weird, but it all cancels out?"

"Pretty much, I think. Till the end, of course."

There came a flash of light from nearby, followed by an instant crack of thunder. The Good Doctor's storm was spreading. Abruptly, the wind shifted, and we were drenched by the sudden pelting.

We bounded across the way immediately, into the shelter of a much larger stone.

Sitting there, miserable in the special way that wetness brings, my gaze was suddenly fixed upon the side of the stone. There, brought out perhaps by the moisture, a series of scratchings and irregularities now appeared to be somewhat more than that.

"Well, I hope the whole gang of them appreciates all this trouble," she said, "Nyarlathotep, Chthulu, and all the rest of the unpronounceables. Makes me wish I had a nice simple job catching mice for some farmer's wife—"

Yes, they were characters in some alphabet I did not know, incised there, worn faint, emphasized suddenly

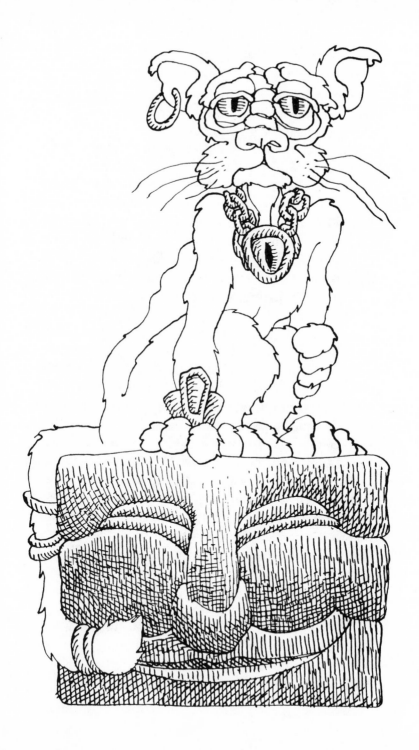

as the trickling water darkened the stone in some places, bringing out contrasts. Even as I watched, they seemed to be growing clearer.

Then I drew back, for they began to glow with a faint red light. They continued to brighten.

"Snuff," she said then, "why're you standing in the rain?" Then her gaze moved to follow my own, and she added, "Uh-oh! Think they heard me?"

Now they were ablaze, those letters, and they began to flow as if reading themselves. Excess light formed itself into a high rectangular perimeter about them.

"I was only joking, you know," she said softly.

The interior of the rectangle took on a milky light. A part of me wanted to bolt and run, but another part stood fascinated by the process. Unfortunately, it was the latter part that seemed to be in control. Graymalk stood like a shadowy statue, staring.

Deep within it then came a roiling, and I suppose it must be called a premonition, for suddenly that other part of me was in control again. I sprang forward, seized Graymalk by the nape of her neck with my teeth and sprang away to the right. Just as I did, a flare of lightning sprang from the rectangle and fell upon the area we had occupied but moments before. I stumbled, feeling a small shock, feeling my hair rise. Graymalk wailed, and the air smelled of ozone.

"I guess they're kind of touchy," I said, rising to my feet and falling again.

Then I felt the wind swirling about us, ten times stronger than it had been earlier. I tried again to get to my feet and was again knocked down. I glanced back at the stone, saw that the roiling had subsided, that another lightning bolt might not be imminent. Instead, a faint outline hung there, of a silver key. I crawled nearer to Graymalk. The wind increased in intensity. Somewhere, a voice came chanting, "Iä! Shub-Niggurath! The Black Goat of the Wood with a Thousand Young!"

"What's happening?" she wailed.

"Someone opened a gate to provide means for expressing disapproval of your remark," I suggested. "That's done now, but the door hasn't swung shut yet. That's what I think."

She leaned against me, back arched, ears flat, fur risen. The wind, stronger still, was pushing against us now, near to the point of irresistibility. I began to slide across the ground in the direction of the gate, dragging her with me.

"I've a feeling it'll close too late!" she cried. "We're going through!"

She turned then and leaped upon me, clinging with all four paws to my neck. Her claws were very sharp.

"We mustn't separate!" she said.

"Agreed!" I choked, as I began sliding faster.

I was able to gather my feet beneath me as we moved. Rather than being pushed through, willy-nilly, some measure of grace might provide a survival edge.

It was easy to stop thinking of it as a rock wall that we were approaching, for there were obvious depths to it, though no clear features presented, and the image of the key had already faded. What lay beyond, I'd no idea; that we were going to go through, I'd no doubt. Better a little dignity then. . . .

Straightening my legs, I leaped forward. Into the breach. Into the mist. . . .

. . . Into the silence. Immediately, as we passed through, the sounds of wind and rainfall ceased. We did not come to rest upon a hard surface, or any other surface. We were suspended in a place of pearl gray light—or, if we fell, there was no sensation of falling. My legs were still extended—forward and back, as if I were leaping a fence—and while misty eddies and currents, faint as high clouds, played about us, my sense of motion was paradoxical; that is, by turning my head in any direction, I could create the feeling of pursuing a different vector.

I did turn my head to the rear in time to see the rectangle fade behind us, paling stones and grass within it. Dotted about the place where it had been, as well as about ourselves, droplets of rain and a few leaves and strands of grass hung in the air. Or perhaps we were all falling together, or rising, depending on—

Graymalk gave a little wail, then looked about. I felt her relax after that, then she said, "It is important that we not be parted here."

"You know where we are?" I asked.

"Yes. I'm sure I will land on my feet, but I don't know about you. Let me move around onto your back. We'll both be more comfortable that way."

She worked her way about my neck then, finally settling into a position behind my shoulders. She did retract her claws as she settled.

"Where," I said, "are we?"

"I see now that something tried to help me as we were being swept forward," she said. "This is not of a piece with the lightning stroke. But the way was opened and he seized it as a means of rescue. Possibly there is even more to it than that."

"I'm afraid I don't understand you," I told her.

"We are between our place and the Dreamworld now," she said.

"You have been here before?"

"Yes, but not *right* here recently."

"It feels as if we could drift here forever."

"I suppose that we could."

"So how do we go ahead—or go back?"

"My memories of this part are all scattered. If we do not like where we find ourselves, we withdraw and try again. I will try it now. Call to me if anything too unnatural occurs."

With that, she grew silent, and while I waited for whatever sequel was to ensue I thought back over the events which had brought us to this place. It struck me as odd that her mere disparaging mention of the Elders had not only been heard, but that whichever had taken umbrage thereby had been strong enough to do something about it. True, the power was rising in this, a most powerful time, but I wondered at such profligacy with it when there must have been multitudes of better uses to which it might be put—unless it were simply another instance of that famous inscrutability which I sometimes think is to be better understood as childishness. Then a possibility struck sparks deep within my mind, but I had to let it go, unexamined, as alterations began about me.

There came a brightening from overhead—nothing as patent as a single light source, but an increasing contrast to the darker area below my feet. I said nothing about it to Graymalk, for I had resolved not to address her—barring emergencies—until she spoke. But I studied that light. There was something familiar about it, from driftings off and awakenings perhaps. . . .

Then I realized it to be an outline, as on a map, of a continent or island—perhaps two or more—hanging there, as in a skiey distance, overhead. This did peculiar things to my orientation, and I struggled to alter my physical relationship to it. I moved my legs and twisted, trying to turn my body so as to look downward rather than up at it.

It was almost too easy, for there followed an immediate turning. The view became clearer, the land masses larger, as we seemed to drift nearer, topographical features resolving themselves against a field of blue, wispy swirls of cloud hung above prominences, along coasts, a pair of large islands surmounted by great peaks between the two greater masses—to the west, if what seemed upward along the vertical axes were indeed north. No reason that it should be, of course, nor, for that matter, that it shouldn't.

Graymalk began to mutter then, in a flat, affectless tone, ". . . To the west of the Southern Sea lie the Basalt Pillars, beyond them the city of Cathuria. East, the coast is green and home to fishers' towns. South, from the black towers of Dylath-Leen is the land of white fungi where the houses are brown and have no windows; beneath the waters there, on still days, one can see the avenue of crippled sphinxes leading to the dome of the great sunken temple. To the north again, one may behold the charnel gardens of Zura, place of unattained pleasures, the templed terraces of Zak, the double headlands of crystal at the harbor of Sona-Nyl, the spires of Thalarion. . . ."

As she spoke we came even nearer, and my attention was taken from spot to spot along the coasts of that sea, those features somehow magnified across the distances, so that I beheld things with the vision of dreaming; though a part of me was baffled by this arcane phenomenon, yet another accepted with a feeling more of memory than discovery.

". . . Dylath-Leen," she mused, "where the wide-mouthed traders with the strange turbans come for their slaves and gold, anchoring black galleys whose stench only the smoking of thagweed can kill, paying with rubies, departing with the powerful oar strokes of invisible rowers. Southwest then to Thran of the sloping alabaster walls, unjoined, and its cloud-catching towers all white and gold, there by the River Shai, wharves all of marble. . . .

"And there lies the granite-walled city of Hlanith, on the shores of the Cerenerian Sea. *Its* wharves are of oak, its houses peaked and gabled. . . .

"There, the perfumed jungle of Kled," she went on, "where lost, ivory palaces sleep undisturbed, once home to monarchs of a forgotten kingdom.

". . . And up the Oukranos River from the Cerenerian Sea slope the jasper terraces of Kiran, where the king of Ilek-Vad comes once a year in a golden palanquin, to pray to the god of the river in the seven-towered temple whence music drifts whenever moonlight falls upon it."

We moved steadily closer as she spoke, drifting now over vast regions—brown, yellow, green. . . .

"... Baharna is eleven days sailing from Dylath-Leen, most important port on the island of Oriab, the great lighthouses Thon and Thal at its harbor's gate, quays all of porphyry. There is its canal to Lake Yath, of the ruined city. It flows through a tunnel with granite doors. The hill-people ride zebras. . . . Westward lies the Valley of Pnoth, amid the peaks of Throk. There the slimy *dholes* burrow among the mountains of bones, cast refuse of ghouls from centuries of their feasting. . . . That peak to the south is Ngranek, two days' ride on zebraback from Baharna, if one would brave the *night-gaunts*. Those who dare Ngranek's slopes will come at last to a vast face carved there, with long-lobed ears and pointed nose and chin. It does not appear to be happy.

"... And back to the northern land, fine Ulthar lies near the River Shai, beyond a great stone bridge in whose arch a living man was sealed when it was built, thirteen hundred years ago. It is a city of neat cottages and cobbled streets where wander cats without number, for the enlightened legislators of long ago laid down laws for our protection. A good, kind village, where travelers take their ease and pet the cats, making much of them, which is as it should be.

"... And there is Urg of the low domes, a stop on the way to Inquanok, frequented by onyx miners. . . .

"... And Inquanok itself, terrible place near the waste of Leng, its houses like palaces with pointed domes and minarets, pyramids, gold walls black with scrolls and swirling with inlays of gold, fluted, arched, capped with gold. Its streets are of onyx, and when the great bell sounds it is answered by the music of horns and viols and chanting voices. High up its central hill lies the massive temple of the Elder Ones, surrounded by its seven-gated garden of pillars, fountains, pools wherein luminous fish sport themselves and reflections of tripods from the temple balcony shimmer and dance. The temple itself bears a great belfry atop its flattened dome, and when the bell sounds masked and hooded priests emerge, bearing steaming bowls to lodges beneath the ground. The Veiled King's palace rises on a nearby hill. He rides forth through bronze gates in a yak-drawn chariot. Beware the father of Shantak-birds who dwells in the temple's dome. Stare too long and he sends you nightmares. Avoid fair Inquanok. No cat may dwell there, for many of its shadows are poison to our kind.

". . . And there is Sarkomand, beyond the Leng Plateau. One mounts salt-covered steps to its basalt walls and docks, temples and squares, column-lined streets, to the place where the sphinx-mounted gates open to its central plaza and two monumental winged lions guard the top of the stairwell leading to the Great Abyss."

We drifted even lower now, and it was as if I could hear the winds that blow between the worlds as she continued her litany of Dreamworld geography.

". . . On the way to Kadath we cross the terrible wasteland of Leng, where, in the great windowless monastery surrounded by monoliths, dwells the High Priest of Dreamworld, his face hidden by a yellow silk mask. His building is older than history, bearing frescoes of the story of Leng; barely human creatures dance amid gone cities, the war with the purple spiders, the landing of the black galleys from the moon. . . .

". . . And we pass Kadath itself, enormous city of ice and mystery, capital of this land. . . .

". . . Coming at last to fair Celephaïs in the land of Ooth-Nargai on the shores of the Cerenerian Sea. . . ."

Now we swooped very low, above a snowcapped peak.

". . . Mount Aran," she intoned, and I saw ginkgo trees upon its lower reaches; then, in the distance, marble walls, minarets, bronze statues. "The Naraxa River joins the sea here. There in the distance lie the Tanarian peaks. That turquoise temple down the Street of Pillars is where the high priest worships Nath-Horthoth. And so we find our way to the place where I have been summoned."

We dropped steadily then, to touch the bright-cut onyx-stone of the street. Immediately, there were sounds about us once again other than the wind, breezes that I could feel. Graymalk leaped from my back, alighting beside me, shook herself, and stared.

"You wander these lands in dreams of catnappery?" I said.

"Sometimes," she replied, "and sometimes elsewhere. And yourself?"

"I think that sometimes I might have."

She turned in a complete circle, paused, then began walking. I followed.

We walked for a long while; none among the merchants and camel drivers or orchid-wreathed priests disturbed our passing.

"There is no time here," she remarked.

"I believe you," I answered, and sailors passed us from the pink-vapored harbor and sunlight sparkled upon the streets, the minarets. I saw no other dogs about, smelled none.

In the distance, a blinding spectacle came into view and we made our way toward it.

"The rose-crystal Palace of the Seventy Delights," she said, "whence he has called."

And so we walked toward it, and it was as if a part of me normally awake were sleeping and part of me normally asleep were awake, a reversal which led to easy acceptance of wonder, to easy forgetting of daylong movements and concerns these past several weeks.

The crystal palace grew before us, gleaming like a piece of pink ice, so that I looked past it rather than directly at it. Our way became more quiet as we approached, and the sun was warm.

When we came into its precincts, I beheld a small, gray form—the only other living thing in sight—sunning itself on the terrace before the palace, head upraised, regarding us. Graymalk led us that way. It proved to be an ancient cat, lying on a square of black onyx.

Drawing near and prostrating herself, she said, "Hail, High Purring One."

"Graymalk, daughter," he answered. "Hello. Rise, please."

She did, saying, "I believe that I felt your presence at the time of an Elder One's wrath. Thank you."

"Yes. I have been watching for all of your month," he said. "You know why."

"I do."

He turned his head, antique yellow eyes meeting my own. I lowered my head out of respect for his venerability, and because Graymalk obviously regarded him as someone of great importance.

"You come in the company of a dog."

"Snuff is my friend," she said. "He pulled me out of a well, cast me back from the Elder One's lightning."

"Yes, I saw him move you when it fell, right before I decided to call you here. He is welcome. Hello, Snuff."

"Hello—sir," I answered.

Slowly, the old cat rose to his feet, arched his back, stretched low, righted himself.

"Times," he said, "are complicated just now. You have entered an unusual design. Come walk with me, daughter, that I may impart a small wisdom concerning the final day. For some things seem too small for the Great Ones' regard, and a cat may know that which the Elder Gods do not."

She glanced at me, and since few can tell when I am smiling, I nodded my head.

They strolled along into the temple itself, and I wondered whether, somewhere, an ancient wolf in a high, craggy place were watching us, always alert, his only message, "Keep watching, Snuff, always." I could almost hear his timeless growl from the places beneath thought.

I sniffed about, waiting. It was hard to tell how long they were gone in a place without time. But it followed that it should not seem to take long. Nor did it.

When I saw them emerge, I wondered again at the strangeness which had paired me in friendship with an opener. And a cat, at that.

Coming up to me, I saw that Graymalk was almost disturbed, or at least puzzled, by the way she raised her right paw and regarded it.

"This way now," the old one stated, and he looked at me as he said it, so I knew that I was included in the invitation.

He led us up an alleyway beside the Palace of Seventy Delights, where fluted dustbins of umber, aquamarine, and russet, their sides inscribed with delicate traceries of black and silver, handles of malachite, jade, porphyry, and chrysoberyl stood, holding forgotten mysteries of the temple. Purple rats fled our approach, and a single lid shivered, emitting a bell-like tone which echoed from the rose-crystal wall.

"In here," he told us, and we followed him into a darkened recess which held a temple postern. Beside it, a less substantial door quivered upon the crystal wall—a churning milkiness beginning within its suddenly apparent rectangle there as we approached.

When we came up before it, he turned to me.

"As you have been a friend of one of my own," he said, "I would give you a boon of knowledge. Ask me anything."

"What does tomorrow hold for me?" I said.

He blinked once.

Then, "Blood," he said. "Seas and messes of it all around you. And you will lose a friend. Go now through the gate."

Graymalk stepped into the rectangle, was gone.

"Thanks, I guess," I said.

"*Carpe baculum!*" he added as I followed, somehow knowing that I recalled a bit of my Latin, and doubtless getting some obscure cat-laugh out of telling me to fetch a stick in a classical language. You get used to little digs from cats about being a dog, though I'd thought their boss might be above that sort of thing. Still, he *is* a cat, and he probably hadn't seen a dog in a long time and just couldn't resist.

"*Et cum spiritu tuo,*" I replied, moving forward and entering.

"*Benedicte,*" I heard his distant response as I drifted again in that place between worlds.

"What was all that business at the end?" Graymalk called back to me.

"He gave me a quick quiz on my Virgil."

"Why?"

"Damned if I know. He's inscrutable, remember?"

Suddenly, she wavered within another rectangle. It was odd, watching her go two-dimensional and ripple that way. Then she turned into a horizontal line, and its ends collapsed upon its middle and she was gone. When my turn came it didn't feel that complicated, though. I joined her atop Dog's Nest before the block of stone, which was again just a stone with some scratches on it. The sun was far into the west, but the storm was over.

I turned in a circle. No one was sneaking up from any direction.

"There's still enough light to check out that spot you located," she said.

"Let's save it for tomorrow. I'm late making my rounds," I told her.

"All right."

We headed homeward. I thought about the old cat's boon, but that wasn't till tomorrow.

"Dognappery's a lot less lush than Celephais," I said, as we walked.

"What's it like?" she asked.

"I'm back in a primal wood with an old wolf named Growler. He teaches me things."

"If there are any Zoogs about," she said, "we passed over your wood to the west of the River Shai. It's below the Gate of Deeper Slumber."

"Maybe," I said, thinking of the small brown creatures who lived in the oaks and fed on the fungi, except when there were people about. Growler laughed at them as he did at most things.

The clouds purpled in the west and our paws grew damp from the grasses. Blood and messes. . . . Perhaps I could use a review.

Tonight Growler and I would ramble, till we fought and I was beat.

October 23

U P IN THE MORNING, OUT ON THE JOB. I hassled the Things, then checked around outside. A black feather lay near our front door. Could be one of Nightwind's. Could be openers on a nasty spell. Could just be a stray feather. I carried it across the road to the field and pissed on it.

Graymalk wasn't about, so I walked over to Larry's place. He let me in and I told him everything that had happened since I'd last seen him.

"We ought to check that hillside," he said. "Could be there'd been a chapel there in the old days."

"True. Want to walk over now?"

"Let's."

I studied his plants while he went for a jacket. There were certainly some exotic ones. I hadn't told him yet about Linda Enderby, perhaps because he'd revealed in passing that all they'd spoken of was botany. Perhaps the Great Detective really was interested in plants.

He returned with his jacket and we went out. It was somewhat blustery when we reached the open fields. At one point we came across a trail of huge misshapen footprints leading off in the direction of the Good Doctor's farmhouse of the perpetual storm. I sniffed at them: Death.

"The big man's been out again," I remarked.

"I haven't been over that way to say hello," Larry said. "I'm beginning to wonder now whether he isn't a rather famous man I've already met, seeking to further his work."

He did not elaborate, as we came upon a crossbow bolt about then, stuck in the bole of a tree.

"What about Vicar Roberts?" I said.

"Ambitious man. I wouldn't be surprised if his aim is to be the only one left standing at the end, sole beneficiary of the opening."

"What about Lynette? This doesn't require a human sacrifice, you know. It just sort of greases the wheels."

"I've been thinking about her," he said. "Perhaps, on the way back, we could go by the vicarage and you could show me which room is hers."

"I don't know that myself. But I'll get Graymalk to show me. Then I'll show you."

"Do that."

We walked on, coming at last to the slopes of the small hill I had determined to be the center.

"So this is the place?" he remarked.

"More or less. Give or take a little, every which way. I don't usually work with maps the way most do."

We wandered a bit then.

"Just your average hillside," he finally said. "Nothing special about it, unless those trees are the remains of a sacred grove."

"But they're saplings. They look like new growth to me."

"Yes. Me, too. I've a funny feeling you're still missing something in the equation. I'm in this version?"

"Yes."

"We've discussed this before. If you take me out of it, where does that move it to?"

"The other side of the hill and farther south and east. Roughly the same distance as from your place to a point across the road from Owen's."

"Let's take a look."

We climbed the hill and climbed back down the other side. Then we walked southeastward.

Finally, we came to a marshy area, where I halted.

"Over that way," I said. "Maybe fifty or sixty paces. I don't see any point in mucking around in it when we can see it from here. It all looks the same."

"Yes. Unpromising." He scanned the area for a time. "Either way, then," he finally said, "you must still be leaving something out."

"A mystery player?" I asked. "Someone who's been lying low all this time?"

"It seems as if there must be. Hasn't it ever happened before?"

I thought hard, recalling Games gone by.

"It's been tried," I said then. "But the others always found him out."

"Why?"

"Things like this," I said. "Pieces that don't fit any other way."

"Well?"

"This is fairly late in the game. It's never gone this long. Everyone's always known everyone else by this time—with only about a week to go."

"In those situations where someone was hiding out, how did you go about discovering him?"

"We usually all know by the Death of the Moon. If something seems wrong afterward that can only be accounted for by the presence of another player, the power is then present to do a divinatory operation to determine the person's identity or location."

"Don't you think it might be worth giving it a try?"

"Yes. You're right. Of course, it's not really my specialty. Even though I know something about all of the operations, I'm a watcher and I'm a calculator. I'll get someone else to give it a try, though."

"Who?"

"I don't know yet. I'll have to find out who's good at it, and then suggest it formally, so that I get to share the results. I'll share them with you then, of course."

"What if it's someone you can't stand?"

"Doesn't matter. There are rules, even if you're trying to kill each other. If you don't follow them, you don't last long. I may have something that that person will want—like the ability to do an odd calculation, say, for something other than the center."

"Such as?"

"Oh, the place where a body will be found. The place where a certain herb can be located. The store that carries a particular ingredient."

"Really? I never knew about those secondary calculations. How hard are they to perform?"

"Some are very hard. Some are easy."

We turned and began walking back.

"How hard's the body-finding one?" he asked as we climbed the hill.

"They're fairly easy, actually."

"What if you tried it for the police officer we put in the river?"

"Now *that* could be tricky, since there are a lot of extra variables involved. If you just misplaced a body, though—or knew that someone had died but didn't know where—that wouldn't be too hard."

"That does sound like a kind of divination," he said.

"When you talk about being an 'anticipator,' of having a pretty good idea of when something's going to happen—or how, or who will be there—isn't that a kind of divination?"

"No. I think it's more a kind of subconscious knack for dealing with statistics, against a fairly well-known field of actions."

"Well, some of my calculations would probably be a lot closer to doing overtly what you seem to do subconsciously. You may well be an intuitive calculator."

"That business about finding the body, though. That smacks of divination."

"It only seems that way to an outsider. Besides, you've just seen what can happen to my calculations if I'm missing some key factor. That's hardly divinatory."

"Supposing I told you that I've had a strong feeling all morning that one of the players has died?"

"That's a little beyond me, I'm afraid. I'd need to know who it was, and some of the circumstances. I really deal more with facts and probabilities than things like that. Are you serious about your feeling?"

"Yes, it's a real anticipation."

"Did you feel it when the Count got staked?"

"No, I didn't. But then, I don't believe he'd technically have been considered living, to begin with."

"Quibble, quibble," I said, and he caught the smile and smiled back. It takes one to know one, I guess.

"You want to show me Dog's Nest? You've gotten me curious."

"Come on," I said, and we went and climbed up to it.

At the top, we walked around a bit, and I showed him the stone we had been sucked through. Its inscription had become barely noticeable scratchings again. He couldn't make them out either.

"Nice view from here, though," he said, turning and studying the land about us. "Oh, there's the manse. I wonder whether Mrs. Enderby's cuttings are taking?"

There was my opening. I could have seized it right then, I suppose, and told him the whole story, from Soho to here. But, at least, I realized then what was holding me back. He reminded me of someone I once knew: Rocco. Rocco was a big, floppy-eared hound, always happy—bouncing about and slavering over life with such high spirits that some found it annoying— and he was very single-minded. I called to him one day on the street and he just dashed across, not even paying puppy-attention to his surroundings. Got run over by a cart. I rushed to his side, and damned if he still didn't seem happy to see me in those final minutes. If I'd kept my muzzle shut he could have stayed happy a lot longer. Now. . . . Well, Larry wasn't stupid like Rocco, but he had a similar capacity for enthusiasm—long frustrated by a big problem, in his case. He seemed on the way to working out some means for dealing with the problem now, and the Great Detective in the guise he had assumed was cheering him up a good deal. Since I didn't really see him as giving much away, I thought of Rocco and said the hell with it. Later.

We climbed down then and headed back, and I let him tell me about tropical plants and temperate plants and arctic plants and diurnal-nocturnal plant cycles and herbal medicines from many cultures. When we neared Rastov's place, I saw at first what appeared a piece of rope hanging from a tree limb, blowing in the wind. A moment later I realized it to be Quicklime, signaling for my attention.

I veered to the left hand side of the road, quickening my pace.

"Snuff! I was looking for you!" he called. "He's done it! He's done it!"

"What?" I asked him.

"Did himself in. I found him hanging when I returned from my foraging. I knew he was depressed. I told you—"

"How long ago was this?"

"About an hour ago," he said. "Then I went to look for you."

"When did you go out?"

"Before dawn."

"He was all right then?"

"Yes. He was sleeping. He'd been drinking last night."

"Are you sure he did it to himself?"

"There was a bottle on a table nearby."

"That doesn't mean anything, the way he'd been drinking."

Larry had halted when he'd seen I was engaged in a conversation. I excused myself from Quicklime to bring him up to date.

"Sounds as if your anticipation was right," I said. "But I couldn't have calculated this one."

Then a thought occurred.

"The icon," I said. "Is it still there?"

"It wasn't anywhere in sight," Quicklime replied. "But it usually isn't, unless he takes it out for some reason."

"Did you check where he normally keeps it?"

"I can't. That would take hands. There's a loose board under his bed. It lies flush and looks normal, but comes up easily for someone with fingers. There's a hollow space beneath it. He keeps it there, wrapped in a red silk bandana."

"I'll get Larry to lift the board," I said. "Is there an unlocked door?"

"I don't know. You'll have to try them. Usually, he keeps them locked. If they are, my window is opened a crack, as usual. You can raise it up and get in that way."

We headed for the house. Quicklime slithered down and followed us.

The front door was unlocked. We entered and waited till Quicklime was beside us.

"Which way?" I asked him.

"Straight ahead, through the door," he said.

We did that, entering a room I had viewed from outside on an earlier inspection. And Rastov hung there, from a rope tied to a rafter, wild black hair and beard framing his pale face, dark eyes bugged, a trickle of blood having run from the left corner of his mouth into his beard, dried now into a dark, scarlike ridge. His face was purple and swollen. A light chair lay on its side nearby.

We studied his remains for only a moment, and I found myself recalling the old cat's remarks from yesterday. Was this the blood he had referred to?

"Where's the bedroom?" I asked.

"Through the door to the rear," Quicklime replied.

"Come on, Larry," I said. "We need you to raise a board."

The bedroom was a mess, with heaps of empty bottles all about. And the bed was disheveled, its linen smelling of stale human sweat.

"There's a loose board under the bed," I said to Larry. To Quicklime, then, "Which board is it?"

Quicklime slipped beneath and halted atop the third one in.

"This one," he said.

"The one Quicklime's showing us," I told Larry. "Raise it, please."

Larry knelt and reached, catching an edge with his fingernails. He found purchase almost immediately and drew it gently upward.

Quicklime looked in. I looked in. Larry looked in. The red bandana was still there, but no three-by-nine-inch piece of wood with an eerie painting on it.

"Gone," Quicklime commented. "It must be somewhere back in the room, with him. We must have missed it."

Larry replaced the board and we returned to the room where Rastov hung. We searched thoroughly, but it did not seem to be present.

"I don't think he killed himself," I said finally. "Somebody overpowered him while he was drunk or hung over, then did that to him. They wanted it to look as if he did it to himself."

"He was pretty strong," Quicklime responded. "But if he'd started in drinking again this morning, he might not have been able to defend himself well."

I relayed our conjectures to Larry, who nodded.

"And the place is so messy you can't really tell whether there was a struggle," he said. "Though, for that matter, the killer could have straightened some furniture afterwards. I'll have to go to the constable. I'll tell him I dropped by, found the door open and walked in. At least, I'd visited here before. It's not as if we'd never met. He won't know we weren't that well acquainted."

"I guess that's best," I told him. Returning my gaze to the corpse, I said, "Can't tell from his clothes either. Looks as if he'd slept in them, more than once."

We moved back to the front room.

"What are you going to do now, Quicklime?" I asked. "You want to move in with Jack and me? That might be simplest, us closers sticking together."

"I think not," he hissed. "I think I'm done with the Game. He was a good man. He took good care of me. He cared about people, about the whole world.

What's that human notion—compassion. He had a lot of that. It's one of the reasons he drank a lot, I think. He felt everybody else's pain too much. No. I'm done with the Game. I'll slip back to the woods now. I still know a few burrows, a few places where the mice make their runs. Leave me alone here for a while now. I'll see you around, Snuff."

"Whatever you think is best, Quicklime," I said. "And if the winter gets too rough, you know where we live."

"I do. Good-bye."

"Good luck."

Larry let me out and we walked back to the road.

"I'll be going this way, then," he said, turning right.

"And I'll be going this way."

I turned left.

"See you soon for the follow-up on this," he said.

"Yes."

I headed home. "And you will lose a friend"—the old cat had said that, too. It had slipped my mind till now.

Jack was not in, and I did the rounds quickly, leaving everything in good order. Stepping outside then, I located his spoor and tracked him to Crazy Jill's.

Graymalk watched me from atop the wall.

"Hello, Snuff," she said.

"Hello, Gray. Jack is here?"

"Yes, he is in having a meal with the mistress. He ran low on supplies and she decided to feed him before their trip."

"Trip?" I asked. "What trip?"

"A shopping trip, into town."

"He did say something about being low on necessaries, and needing to visit the market soon. . . ."

"Yes. So he's sent for a coach. It should be here in an hour or so. It will be exciting to see the town again."

"You're going, too?"

"We're all going. The mistress also needs some things."

"Shouldn't we stay behind to guard the places?"

"The mistress has a very good daylong warding spell, which she will share. It will also capture likenesses of attempted trespassers. I understand that a part of the reason we are going this way is to see whether anyone tries such a thing. Everyone will see our coach go by. On our return, we may learn who are our most important enemies."

"This was decided recently, I take it?"

"Just this morning, while you were out."

"This may be a good time for it," I acknowledged, "with the big event only a week from tomorrow— and in light of the way things have been going."

"Oh?" She rose, stretched, and jumped down from the wall. "There are new developments?"

"Walk with me," I said.

"Where?"

"To the vicarage. You said we have an hour."

"All right."

We left the yard, headed south.

"Yes," I told her as we went, "we've lost the mad monk," and I recounted the morning's events.

"And you think the vicar did it?" she asked.

"Probably. He seems our most militant player. But

that's not why I wanted to visit his focus. I just wanted to learn the location of the room where he keeps Lynette a prisoner."

"Of course," she said. "If he has the Count's ring and the Alhazred Icon as well as the pentacle bowl, he could do some pretty nasty things between now and next week. You said they mainly increased his technical prowess, and I thought you meant for the ceremony. But he could hurt people with them right now. I asked the mistress."

"Well, that's technical."

"But you acted as if it weren't important."

"I still don't think it is. He'd be a fool to use the actual tools that way, when he should be relying on his own abilities. The tools have a way of producing repercussive effects when they're used extracurricularly. He could wind up hurting himself badly unless he's a real master, and I don't think he is."

"How can you be sure?"

"I doubt a master would run around with a crossbow, shooting at bats, or plan a human sacrifice when it's not absolutely necessary—just to be safe. He's insecure in his power. A master aims at economy of operations, not proliferation."

"That sounds right, Snuff. But if he's too insecure mightn't he be tempted to try an operation with the tools against the rest of us, anyway—just to narrow the field and make things easier for himself later on?"

"If he's that foolish, the results are on his own head."

"And the person he directs the power against, don't forget that. It could be you."

"I understand you're safe if your heart is pure."

"I'll try to remember that."

When we reached the vicarage she led me around to the rear.

"Up there," she said, looking at a window directly overhead. "That's her room."

"I've never seen her about," I said.

"I gather from Tekela that she's been locked up for several weeks."

"I wonder how securely?"

"Well, she hasn't come out, to my knowledge. And I told you I saw a chain around her ankle."

"How thick?"

"That's hard to say. You want me to climb up and take another look?"

"Maybe. I wonder whether the vicar is in?"

"We could check the stable, see whether his horse is there."

"Let's do that."

So we headed to the small stable in the rear and entered there. There were two stalls, and both were empty.

"Off on a call," she said.

"What do you want?" came a voice from the rafters.

Looking up, I beheld the albino raven.

"Hello, Tekela," Graymalk said. "We were just passing by, and wanted to see whether you'd heard the news about Rastov."

There followed a moment's silence, then, "What about Rastov?"

"He's dead," Graymalk said. "Hanged."

"And what of the snake?"

"Gone back to the woods."

"Good. I never liked snakes. They raid nests, eat eggs."

"Have you any news?"

"Only that the big man has been about again. There was an argument at the farmhouse and he went out to the barn for a time and crouched in a corner. The Good Doctor went after him and there was more argument. He ran off into the night then. Went back later, though."

"That's interesting. I wonder what it was about."

"I don't know."

"Well, we'll be going now. Good-bye."

"Yes."

We departed and returned to the vicarage. Graymalk looked back.

"She can't see us from that rafter," she said. "Do you want me to climb up?"

"Wait," I said. "I want to try a trick I learned from Larry."

I approached the back door and I checked the stable again. I could see no flash of white.

Rising onto my hind legs, I put a paw against the door for balance, held it a moment, then dropped it to join the other in pressing on the knob toward its center. I turned my body as I made the effort. I had to try three times, adjusting my grip. The third time it went far enough to make a clicking sound and my weight caused the door to swing inward. I dropped into a normal position and entered.

"That's quite a trick," she said, following me. "Do you feel any wards?"

"No."

I pushed the door almost shut with my shoulder. It had to be paw-openable, quickly, on our return.

"Now what?" she asked.

"Let's find the stairway. I'd like to see how the girl is secured."

We stopped in the study on the way and she showed me the bowl and its skull. The bowl was indeed the real thing. I'd seen it many times before. Neither the icon nor the ring lay in such plain sight, however, and I hadn't the time to try my skills on drawers. We returned to our search for a stair.

It was located along the west wall. We mounted it, and Graymalk led me to Lynette's room. The door was closed, but it did not seem necessary that it be locked, with her chained up.

I tried the door trick again and it worked the first time. I'd have to see whether Larry had any other good ones. . . .

As we entered, Lynette's eyes widened, and she said, "Oh."

"I'll go rub up against her and let her pet me," Graymalk said. "That makes people happy. You can be looking at the chain while I do that."

It was actually the locks in which I was most interested. But even as I advanced to do that I heard the distant clopping of a horse's hoofs, approaching at a very rapid pace.

"Uh-oh," Graymalk said amid purrings, as the girl stroked her and told her how pretty she was. "Tekela must have seen us come in, flew off and given alarm."

I went through with my inspection. The chain was heavy enough to do its job, and the lock that secured it to the bed frame was impressively heavy. The one which fastened it to Lynette's ankle was smaller, but still hardly a thing to be dealt with in a moment.

"I know enough," I said, as the hoofbeats came up beside the house, turned the corner, and I heard a horse blowing heavily.

"Race you home!" Graymalk said, leaping to the floor and running for the stair.

The rider was dismounting as we bounded to the first floor. A second or two later I heard the back door open, then slam.

"Bad," Graymalk said. Then, "I can occupy the vicar."

"The hell with him! I'm going to take out the study window!"

I reached the corner just as the nasty little man came around the other corner, a riding crop in his hand. I had to slow to turn into the room and he brought it down across my back. Before he could strike a second time, though, Graymalk had leaped into his face, all of her claws extended.

I bounded across the room, a scream rising at my back, and leaped at the window, closing my eyes as I hit. I took the thing with me, mullions and all. Turning then, I sought Graymalk.

She was nowhere in sight but I heard her yowl from within. Two bounds and a leap brought me back into the room. He was holding her high by her hind legs and swinging the crop. When it connected she screamed and he let her fall, for he had not expected me to return, let alone be coming at him low off the floor with my ears flat and a roar in my throat straight from my recent refresher with Growler.

He swung the crop but I came in beneath it. If

Graymalk were dead, I was going to kill him. But I heard her call out, "I'm leaving!" as I struck against his chest, knocking him over backward.

My jaws were open and his throat had been my target. But I heard her going out the window, and I turned my head and bit hard, hearing cartilage crunch as I drew my teeth along through his right ear. Then I was off of him, across the room, and following Graymalk outside to the sounds of his screams.

"Want to ride on my back?" I called to her.

"No! Just keep going!"

We ran all the way home.

As we lay there in the front yard, me panting and her licking herself, I said, "Sorry I got you into that, Gray."

"I knew what I was doing," she said. "What did you do to him there at the end?"

"I guess I mangled his ear."

"Why?"

"He hurt you."

"I've been hurt worse than that."

"That doesn't make it right."

"Now you have a first-class enemy."

"Fools have no class."

"A fool might try the tools against you. Or something else."

I interrupted my panting to sigh. Just then a bird-shaped shadow slid across us. Looking up, I was not surprised to see Tekela go by.

After lunch and a quick running of my rounds the coach came by, and we all entered and embarked for town. It had room for me to sit beside a window while Graymalk curled up on the seat across from me. Master and mistress faced each other to my right, chatting, beside a window of their own. I'd received only a few minor cuts from the glass, but Graymalk had a nasty welt along her right side. My heart did not feel pure when I thought of the vicar.

I watched the sky. Before we'd gone a mile I caught sight of Tekela again. She circled above the coach, then swooped low for a look inside. Then she was gone. I did not awaken Graymalk to remark upon it.

The sky was cloudy, and a wind occasionally buffeted the coach. When we passed the Gipsies' camp there was small activity within and no music. I listened to the horses clop along, muttering about the ruts and the driver's propensity to lay on the lash at the end of a long day. I was glad I wasn't a horse.

After a long while we came to the bridge and crossed over. I looked out across the dirty waters and wondered where the officer had gotten to. I wondered whether he had a family.

As we moved along Fleet Street to the Strand and then down Whitehall, I caught occasional glimpses of an albino raven, variously perched, watching. We made several stops for purchases along the way, and finally, when we disembarked in Westminster, site of many a midnight stroll, Jack said to me, "Let's meet back here in about an hour and a half. We've a few esoteric purchases to make." This was fine with me, as I enjoy wandering city streets. Graymalk took me to see the mews where she'd once hung out.

We spent the better part of an hour strolling, sorting through collected smells, watching the passersby.

Then, in an alley we'd chosen for a shortcut, I had a distinct feeling halfway down its length, that something was wrong. This came but moments before the compact figure of the vicar emerged from a recessed doorway, a bulging bandage upon his ear, lesser dressings covering his cheeks. Tekela rode upon his shoulder, her white merging with that of the bandages, giving to his head a grotesque, lopsided appearance. She must have been giving him directions as to our movements. I showed them my teeth and kept moving. Then I heard a footfall behind me. Two men with clubs had sprung from another doorway and were already upon me, swinging them. I tried to turn upon them, but it was too late. I heard the vicar laugh right before one of the bludgeons fell upon my head. My last sight was of Graymalk, streaking back up the alley.

I awoke inside a dirty cage, a sickening smell in my nose, my throat, my lungs. I realized that I had been given chloroform. My head hurt, my back hurt. I drew and expelled several deep breaths to clear my breathing apparatus. I could hear whimpers, growls, a pathetic mewing, and faint, sharp barks of pain from many directions. When my sense of smell began to work again, all manner of doggy and catty airs came to me. I raised my head and looked about and wished I hadn't.

Mutilated animals occupied cages both near and far—dogs and cats without tails or the proper number of legs, a blind puppy whose ears had been cut off, a cat missing large patches of her skin, raw flesh showing at which she licked, mewing constantly the while. What mad place was this? I checked myself over quickly, to make certain I was intact.

At the room's center was an operating table, a large tray of instruments beside it. On hooks next to the door across the way hung a number of once-white laboratory coats with suspicious-looking stains upon them.

As my head cleared my memory returned to me, and I realized what had happened. The vicar had delivered me into the hands of a vivisectionist. At least Graymalk had escaped. That was something.

I inspected the door to my cage. It was a simple enough latch that held it shut, but the mesh was too fine for me to reach through and manipulate it. And the mesh was too tough to be readily breached by tooth or claw. What would Growler counsel? Things were a lot simpler in the primeval wood.

The most obvious plan was to fake lassitude when they came for me, then to spring to attack as soon as the cage door was opened. I'd a feeling, though, that I wasn't the first ever to think of such a ploy, and where were the others now? Still, I couldn't just lie there and contribute to medical understanding. So unless something better came along I resolved to give this plan a try when they came for me.

When they did, of course, they were ready. They'd a lot of expertise with fangs and knew just how to go about it. There were three of them, and two had on elbow-length padded gloves. When I pulled the awake, lunge, and bite maneuver I got a padded fore-arm forced back between my jaws, and my legs were seized and held while someone twisted an ear pain-fully. They were very efficient, and they had me strapped to the table in less than a minute. I wondered just how long I had been unconscious.

I listened to their conversation as they began their preparations:

"Strange, 'im payin' us so well to do a job on this 'un," said the one who had twisted my ear.

"Well, it is a strange job, and it does involve some extra work," said the one who was arranging the instruments into neat little rows. "Bring over some clean parts buckets. He was very specific that when we render him down, a piece at a time, for candles, there be no foreign blood or other materials mixed in."

" 'Ows 'e to know?"

"For what he's paying he can have it his way."

"I'll 'ave to scrub 'em out."

"Do it."

A brief reprieve, to the sound of running water, followed, drowning out some of the whimpers and cries which were beginning to get to me.

"And where's the cask for his head?"

"I left it in t'other room."

"Get it. I want everything to hand. Nice doggy." He patted my head as we waited. The muzzle they'd gotten onto me prevented my expressing my opinion.

"He was a strange one," said the third man—a thin, blond fellow with very bad teeth—who had been silent till then. "What's special about doggy candles?"

"Don't know and don't care," said the one who had patted me—a large, beefy man with very blue eyes—

and he returned his attention to his instruments. "We give a customer what he pays for."

The other returned then—a short man with wide shoulders, large hands, and a tic at the corner of his mouth. He bore what looked like an odd-sized lunch pail. "I have it now," he said.

"Good. Then gather round for a lesson."

Then I heard it—*Dzzp!*—a high-pitched whine descending to a low throb in about three seconds each cycle. It is above the range of the human ear, and it accompanies the main curse, circling at a range of about a hundred fifty yards initially. *Dzzp!*

"First, I will remove the left rear leg," began the beefy man as he reached for a scalpel.

Dzzp!

The others drew near, reaching after other instruments and holding them ready for him.

Dzzp! The circle might well be smaller by now, of course.

There came a loud pounding upon an outer door.

"The devil!" said the beefy man.

"Shall I see who 'tis?" asked the smaller man.

"No. We're operating. He can come back if it's important."

Dzzp!

It came again, more heavily; this time it was obviously the sound of someone kicking upon the door.

"Inconsiderate lout!"

"Ruffian!"

"Churl!"

Dzzp!

The third time that the knocking occurred it seemed

as if each blow were performed by a strong man striking his shoulder against the door, attempting to break it down.

"What cheek!"

"Per'aps I should 'ave words with 'im."

"Yes, do."

The shorter man took a single step toward the entrance when a splintering sound reached us from the next room, followed by a loud crash.

Dzzp!

Heavy footsteps crossed the outer room. Then the door immediately across from me was flung open. Jack stood upon the threshold, staring at the cages, the vivisectionists, myself upon the table. Graymalk peered in from behind him.

"Just who do you think you are, bursting into a private laboratory?" said the beefy man.

". . . Interrupting a piece of scientific research?" said the tall man.

". . . And damaging our door?" said the short man with the wide shoulders and large hands.

Dzzp!

I could see it now, like a black tornado, surrounding Jack, settling inward. If it entered him completely he would no longer be in control of his actions.

"I've come for my dog," he said. "That's him on your table."

He moved forward.

"No, you don't, laddie," said the beefy man. "This is a special job for a special client."

"I'll be taking him and leaving now."

The beefy man raised his scalpel and moved around the table.

"This can do amazing things to a man's face, pretty boy," he said.

The others picked up scalpels, also.

"I'd guess you've never met a man as really knows how to cut," the beefy one said, advancing now.

Dzzp!

It was into him, and that funny light came into his eyes, and his hand came out of his pocket and captured starlight traced the runes on the side of his blade.

"Well-met," Jack said then, through the teeth of his grin, and he continued to walk straight ahead.

When we left I realized that the old cat had been right about the seas and messes, too. I wondered what sort of light they would give.

October 24

HEN THE WARDS WERE REMOVED YESTERDAY evening they showed that Nightwind had been by at dusk, trying to peer in. Also, Cheeter. And a huge, lean wolfish-looking creature. And the Things were all still held by their restraints, though struggling enthusiastically. I was feeling a little worse for my usage, but I forced a spring into my step and went and strolled past the church. Tekela was perched atop it and she stirred and studied me as I went by, but we exchanged no words. As soon as I was past, though, I glanced back and saw that she was gone. Good. I went home and slept.

This morning, I learned from Larry that Mrs. Enderby had run off to town as soon as word of Rastov's death became current. Later in the day, the Great Detective had shown up to view the remains and the premises. I brought Larry up to date on everything that had happened after I'd left him, and he assured me that he had not been by the house last night. He told me that he intended to rescue Lynette, but that she was safe enough for now. If he freed her too early there would be pursuit both physical and nonphysical, now the power was rising strongly; and more importantly, there would be time for the vicar to make other plans, jeopardizing some unknown innocent. The timing, he said, would be very important. Weakening the vicar this way, he decided, could well be his main part in things. I told him that I'd help any way I could. I rested a lot afterwards and visited with Graymalk.

It began to rain late that night, a steady drizzle. Jack was in his laboratory, distilling essences or something like that. I had spoken with him last night, of course, between midnight and one, keeping him current on all particulars of my adventures.

"Isn't your association with Jill a little—awkward—this far along in the Game?" I'd said, near to one o'clock.

"Strictly professional," he had replied. "Besides, she's a good cook. And what about you and the cat?"

"We get along well," I'd said. "Any chance of your getting Jill to change her mind about opening?"

"I don't think so," he'd answered.

"She's not making you think about switching, I hope?"

"Of course not!"

"Well, if I may speak freely—"

The clock struck one and I couldn't.

I watched the darkened windows flood for a while, made my rounds, and slept some more.

When all hell breaks loose in our vicinity, it does it

with style. I was awakened by an enormous thunder-clap, sounding as if it had occurred just overhead; and the brightness of the lightning stroke had been visible through my closed eyelids. Suddenly, I was on my feet in the front hall, not certain how I had gotten there. Along with the echoes of the crash, however, my mind held memory of the sounds of breaking glass.

The mirror had shattered. The Things were slithering out.

I began barking immediately.

I heard an exclamation from the room where Jack worked, followed by the sound of some instrument or book being dropped. Then the door opened and he was hurrying toward me. When he saw the slitherers he called to me, "Snuff, find a container!" and he returned to the laboratory, where I heard a cabinet opened.

I looked about. I raced into the parlor, slitherers spreading like a slow tidal wave at my back. Upstairs, the Thing in the Steamer Trunk began beating upon its confines with frantic exertion. I heard wood splinter as it struck. And there were rattles from the attic. Another flash created a moment of yellow day beyond the windows, and the thunderclap that came with it shook the house.

There was nothing in the parlor in the way of a mirror, but on a side table near the door stood a partly full (partly empty?) bottle of port wine, of the ruby variety. Recalling that this species casts a spell within the bottle, I reared and pushed it off of the table with my paw, so that it fell upon a rug rather than the floor's wood. It did not shatter, and its cork remained in place. There came another flash and another crash. The Things Upstairs continued their noisy activity, with indication that at least the inhabitant of the steamer trunk had gotten free. A glance hallward showed me the steady, continuous exodus of the Things from the Mirror. I heard Jack's footfalls. An uncanny glow began to fill the room and the hall and it did not seem entirely attributable to the internal incandescence of the slitherers.

Rolling the bottle hallward, I saw Jack standing at the hall's far end, a wand in his hand. It was the no-nonsense wand he had used to transfer the slitherers from mirror to mirror earlier, and not the powerful Game artifact—the Closing Wand—which was also in his possession. While he is master of the Knife (or vice-versa), the Knife is not, technically, a Game tool, though it may be used as a part of the Game. The Knife is the embodiment of his curse as well as a special source of power. He saw me and he saw the bottle at the same time that I saw him.

Jack raised the wand and used it to part the flowing mass which separated us. Then he came forward and it slithered closed behind him as he advanced. Coming up beside me, he picked up the bottle then, held it in his left hand and uncorked it with his teeth. There came another thunder roll and the eerie lighting assumed a definite greenish cast, giving Jack a corpselike appearance.

There was a scrambling sound overhead, and the yellow-eyed Thing from the Steamer Trunk bounded down the stair, cracking the banister as it came.

"Deal with it, Snuff!" Jack cried. "I can't!" and he turned his attention and his wand upon the Things from the Mirror, compelling the nearest to enter the bottle.

I gathered myself and sprang across the flow of slitherers, moving to the foot of the stair, my lips curled back and hair bristling as the Thing came down. Too bad its neck was so short. I knew I was going to have to tear out its throat. The green light hung about it and the rain sounded like thrown gravel against the roof and windows. The Thing spread its arms—ending in very nasty talons—very wide, and I knew that I had to move immediately, in and out, and accomplish it in a matter of seconds if I were to emerge relatively unscathed—which I would need to be, to help deal with the sequel, which, even now, I could hear scrambling down the attic stair. The lightning flashed again. I roared to the accompaniment of thunder as I launched myself at an awkward angle.

I struck the wall on my way down, for the Thing's arm struck me after my jaws had closed like a trap and I'd applied torque with my entire body, crunching and tearing away at its gullet before I let go to drop back. It was the arm and not the talons that connected with me, though. I dropped, momentarily senseless, to the floor, a terrible taste in my mouth, as the Thing from the Attic came into sight at the head of the stair and commenced its descent.

Seeing the Thing from the Steamer Trunk reeling and clutching at its throat, dripping steaming juices, the Thing from the Attic slowed for a moment, regarding the carnage. Then it rushed downward.

I pulled myself to my feet, preparing to face it as it thrust the reeling one aside and came on. Instead, though, the dying one seemed to take its descent as

another attack, swung toward it, and raked it with its talons. The Thing from the Attic seized it, snarling, and bit at its twisted face. At my back, I could hear Jack moving about, bottling slitherers. A moment later, the banister gave way, and the pair on the stair were in the air.

Lightning flashed again, and again, and again, thunder coming and staying, becoming its steady accompaniment; and yet more flashes walked through the sky, entered at the windows, fluoresced the ubiquitous green to an eye-piercing intensity. The sounds of the rain were submerged. The house began to shudder and creak. Copies of *The Strand Magazine* fluttered floorward from the mantel. Pictures fell from the walls, sets of Dickens and Surtees from their shelves; vases, candelabra, glasses, and trays slid from tables; plaster descended like snow from the ceiling. Prince Albert stared at the blizzard through cracked glass. Martin Farquhar Tupper lay atop Elizabeth Barrett Browning, their covers torn.

When the Thing from the Attic rose—shaking its head, rolling its eyes, casting wild glances about—the other lay still upon the floor, steam still rising from its scaly throat, head twisted to its left.

I seemed to hear Growler, prompting me to try for the throat again, and I slashed forward, attempting to repeat my earlier move.

I missed my target as it drew back, attempting, belatedly, to grapple me to it. My impact staggered it, however, and I slashed its left shoulder as I fell.

Immediately, as I secured my footing, I seized its right leg above the ankle and ground down for a bone-cruncher of a bite. It recovered quickly and kicked me with the other foot. I hung on for another second's damage before releasing it and scrambling away, able to ride with the second kick. One, I figured I could take in trade for something that would slow its movements. But I lack the bulldog sensibility as well as the physique.

The lightning and thunder had continued steadily the entire while—the thunder now having achieved the state of a continuous roaring, as of a tornado singing its deep-throated song about the house—and the intensity of the light had us moving through a tableau of green and black, where tiny sparks now danced upon the surfaces of everything metallic, and all of my hair was on end for reasons other than the stimulus of combat. It was obvious now that this was no normal storm but a manifestation of magical attack.

I tried for the Thing's other ankle and missed. Turning, I slashed at the arm which swung at me. I missed that, too, but it missed me, also.

I darted away, growling, roared and feinted to its right. It put weight on the injured ankle to reach after me and went off balance, struggled to recover. I was behind it immediately, passing on that side, and worrying the ankle again, from the rear.

It bellowed then as it tried to reach me, but I hung on until, finally, it cast itself over backwards in an attempt to fall upon and crush me. I relaxed my hold and tried to move away as it did so, but a flailing arm struck me on the head, knocking me to the floor, doubling my vision.

Therefore, it was two Jacks that I saw, wielding two blades, piercing two monsters' throats.

Even as I crawled out from beneath the Attic Thing's

outflung arm, the basement door crashed open, and in several quick bounds the Thing from the Circle was upon me.

"Now, hound, I eat you!" it said.

I shook my head, trying to clear it.

"Snuff! Get back!" Jack told me, turning toward it.

Dzzp!

The starlight danced upon the blade in his hand, and I needed no further persuasion. I crawled toward the farther end of the now slitherless hall, passing a corked bottle of port and spirits as I went. Pieces of mirror gave back green dogs with jagged edges.

Dzzp!

I watched as Jack finished his business, ready in case he required assistance, grateful that he did not.

Plaster continued to rain down. Everything loose was on the floor. The thunder and the light and the house's shuddering had almost become a part of the environment. I suppose that if you lived with it long enough, there might come a time when you stopped noticing. I didn't really want to wait and see.

As I watched the Thing from the Circle finally fall, following a masterful upstroke, I turned my stronger emotions toward the perpetrator of the onslaught which had caused their release. It was more than merely annoying, having had to put up with them all these weeks and then to lose them this way before they could fulfill their function. Under the proper constraints, they had been intended as the bodyguard for our retreat, should one be necessary, following the events of the final night—after which they would have had their freedom in some isolated locale, obtaining the opportunity to add to the world's folklore of a darker nature. Now, ruined, the buffer plan. They weren't essential, but they might have proved useful should we have to exit pursued by Furies.

When the business was done, Jack traced pentagrams with his blade, calling upon the powers that would cleanse the place. With the first one, the green glow faded; with the second, the house stopped its shuddering; with the third, the thunder and lightning went away; with the fourth, the rain ceased.

"Good show, Snuff," he said then.

There came a knocking on the back door. We both headed in that direction, the blade vanishing and Jack's hair and clothing getting rearranged along the way.

He opened the door. Jill and Graymalk stood before us.

"Are you all right?" Jill asked.

Jack smiled, nodded, and stepped aside.

"Won't you come in?" he said.

They did, though not before I'd noted that it seemed perfectly dry outside.

"I'll invite you into the parlor," Jack said, "if you don't mind stepping over a few dismembered ogres."

"Never did before," the lady answered, and he led her in that direction.

The parlor floor was full of what had been on the shelves, the tables, the mantelpiece, and everything was powdered with plaster. Jack raised the sofa cushions one by one, punching each and turning it upside-down before replacing it. She took the seat he offered her, which afforded a view of the broken mirror and slashed demonic carcasses sprawled in the hall.

The clock chimed 11:45.

"I'll have to offer you sherry," Jack said. "The port's gone bad."

"Sherry will be fine."

He repaired to the cabinet, fetching back two glasses and a bottle. After he had poured a pair and given her one he raised the other and looked at her over it.

"What prompts your visit?" he asked.

"I hadn't seen you in over an hour," she replied, taking a small sip of sherry.

"That is true," he answered, sipping his own. "But it is often that way with us. Every day, in fact. Still. . . ."

"I refer to your house as well as your person. I heard a small sound earlier—as of the tinkling of a crystal bell—from this direction. When I looked this way I saw nothing but a well of impenetrable darkness."

"Ah, the old crystal bell effect," he mused. "Haven't seen that one since Alexandria. So you didn't hear any thunder, see any lightning?"

"Not at all."

"Not badly done then, though I hate to admit it," he said, taking another sip.

"Was it the vicar?"

"I'd guess. Most likely still irritated with Snuff here."

"Perhaps you should have a few words with him."

"I don't believe in giving warnings. But I give anybody two attempts on us, to discover their folly. If they do not, and they try a third time, I kill them. That's all."

"He sent those creatures after you?" She gestured toward the hall.

"No," he replied. "They were my own. They got loose during the attack. It must have involved a general manumission spell. Pity. I had better use for the fellows than this."

She set down her glass, rose, visited the hall, and inspected them. She returned a little later.

"Impressive," she said. "What they are, and what got done to them." She seated herself again. "What I'm wondering most, though, is what you're going to do with them now."

"Hm," he said, toying with his glass. "It's rather far to the river."

I nodded vigorously.

"I suppose I could just stow them in the basement, throw a piece of canvas over them, or something like that."

"They might start to smell pretty bad."

"They already smell pretty bad."

"True. But it would be awkward if they were discovered on the premises, and when they start to decompose it might lead someone official this way."

"Conceded. I suppose I could just dig a big hole somewhere and bury them."

"You wouldn't want to do it around here, and they look too husky to lug far."

"You've a point there. Have *you* any ideas?"

"No," she said, sipping her sherry.

I barked once and they looked at me. I glanced at the clock. It was approaching midnight.

"I think Snuff has a suggestion," she said.

I nodded.

"He'll have to wait a few minutes."

"*I* can't," Graymalk said to me suddenly.

"Cats are that way," I replied.

"What do you want to do with them?"

"I say we take them over to Owen's place and stuff them into some of his wicker baskets. Then we haul them up into the big oak tree, set fire to them, and run like hell."

"Snuff, that's grotesque."

"Glad you like it, too," I said. "And it makes for a great Halloween gag, even if it is a little early."

The clock struck twelve.

The humans bought my idea; and we went out to do it. And ah, my foes, and oh, my friends, they gave a lovely light.

Hickory-dickory-dock.

October 25

JILL CAME BACK TO OUR PLACE AFTERWARDS, last night, and helped to straighten things. Graymalk and I slipped out while they were drinking another sherry and hit it over to the vicarage. The study was illuminated and Tekela was perched on the roof beside the chimney, head beneath her wing.

"Snuff, I'm going after that damned bird," Graymalk said.

"I don't know that it's good form, Gray, doing something like that right now."

"I don't care," she said, and she disappeared.

I waited and watched, for a long while. Suddenly, there was a flurry on the roof. There came a rattle of claws, a burst of feathers, and Tekela took off across the night, cawing obscenities.

Graymalk descended at the corner and returned.

"Nice try," I said.

"No, it wasn't. I was clumsy. She was fast. Damn."

We headed back.

"Maybe you'll give her a few nightmares, any-way."

"That'd be nice," she said.

Growing moon. Angry cat. Feather on the wind. Autumn comes. The grass dies.

The morning dealt us a hand in which last night's small irony was seen and raised. Graymalk came scratching on the door and when I went out she said, "Better come with me."

So I did.

"What's it about?" I asked.

"The constable and his assistants are at Owen's place, investigating last night's burnings."

"Thanks for getting me," I said. "Let's go and watch. It should be fun."

"Maybe," she said.

When we got there I understood the intimation in her word. The constable and his men paced and measured and poked. The remains of the baskets and the remains which had been in the baskets were now on the ground. There were, however, the remains of four baskets and their contents rather than the three I remembered so well.

"Oh-oh," I said.

"Indeed," she replied.

I considered the inhuman remains of the three and the very human remains of the fourth.

"Who?" I asked.

"Owen himself. Someone stuffed him into one of his baskets and torched it."

"A brilliant idea," I said, "even if it was plagiarized."

"Go ahead and mock," said a voice from overhead. "He wasn't your master."

"Sorry, Cheeter," I said. "But I can't come up with a lot of sympathy for a man who tried to poison me."

"He had his crochets," the squirrel admitted, "but he also had the best oak tree in town. An enormous number of acorns were ruined last night."

"Did you see who got him?"

"No. I was across town, visiting Nightwind."

"What will you do now?"

"Bury more nuts. It's going to be a long winter, and an outdoor one."

"You could join MacCab and Morris," Graymalk observed.

"No. I think I'll follow Quicklime's example and call it quits. The Game is getting very dangerous."

"Do you know whether whoever did it took Owen's golden sickle?" I asked.

"It's not around out here," he said. "It could still be inside, though."

"You have a way in and out, don't you?"

"Yes."

"Had he a special place he kept it?"

"Yes."

"Would you go inside and check and tell us whether it's still there?"

"Why should I?"

"There might be something you'd like from us one day—a few scraps, the chasing away of a predator. . . ."

"I'd rather have something right now," he said.

"What's that?" I asked.

He leaped, but instead of falling he seemed to drift down to land beside us.

"I didn't know you were a flying squirrel," Graymalk said.

"I'm not," he replied. "That's a part of it, though."

"I don't understand," she told him.

"I was a pretty dumb nut-chaser until Owen found me," he said. "Most squirrels are. We know what we have to do to stay in business, but that's about it. Not like you guys. He made me smarter. He gave me special things I can do, too, like that glide. But I lost something for it. I want to trade all this in and go back to being what I was—a happy nut-chaser who doesn't care about opening and closing."

"What all's involved?" I asked.

"I gave up something for all this, and I want it back."

"What?"

"Look down at the ground around me. What do you see?"

"Nothing special," Graymalk said.

"My shadow's gone. He took it. And he can't give it back now, because he's dead."

"It's a pretty cloudy day," Graymalk said. "It's hard to tell. . . ."

"Believe me. I ought to know."

"I do," I said. "It'd be a silly thing to go on about this way, otherwise. But what's so important about a shadow? Who cares? What good is it to you up there, anyway, jumping around in trees where you can't even see it most of the time?"

"There's more to it than that," he explained. "It's attached to other things that go away with it. I can't feel things the way that I used to. I used to just know things—where the best nuts were, what the weather was going to be like, where the ladies were when the time came, how the seasons were changing. Now I think about it, and I can figure all these things out and can make plans to take advantage of them—something I could never have done before. But I've lost all those little feelings that came with the kind of knowing that comes without thinking. And I've—thought—about it a lot. I miss them. I'd rather go back to them than think and soar the way I do. You understand about magic. Not too many people do. I'll check on the sickle if you'll break Owen's shadow-spell for me."

I glanced at Graymalk, who shook her head.

"I've never heard of that spell," she said.

"Cheeter, there are all kinds of magical systems," I said. "They're just shapes into which the power is poured. We can't know them all. I've no idea what Owen did to your shadow or your—intuition, I guess, and the feelings that go with it. Unless we had some idea where it is and how to go about returning it and restoring it to you, I'm afraid we can't be of help."

"If you can get into the house, I can show it to you," he said.

"Oh," I said. "What do you think, Gray?"

"I'm curious," she told me.

"How do we go about it?" I asked. "Any open windows? Unlocked doors?"

"You couldn't fit in through my opening. It's just a little hole, up in the attic. The back door is usually unlocked, but it takes a human to open it."

"Maybe not," Graymalk said.

"We will have to wait till the constable and his men are gone," I said.

"Of course."

We waited, hearing the puzzlement over the unnatural remains of the three repeated many times. A doctor came and looked and shook his head and took notes and departed, after deciding that there was only one human body—Owen's—and promising to file a report in the morning. Mrs. Enderby and her companion stopped by and chatted with the constable for a time, glancing at Graymalk and me almost as much as at the remains. She left before too long, and the remains were sacked and labeled and hauled away in a cart, along with what remained of the baskets, which were also labeled.

As the cart creaked away, Graymalk, Cheeter, and I glanced at each other. Then Cheeter flowed up the bole of a tree, drifted from its top to that of another, then over to the roof of the house.

"It would be nice to be able to do that," Graymalk remarked.

"It would," I agreed, and we headed for the back door.

I rose as before, clasped the knob tightly and twisted. Almost. I tried again, a little harder, and it yielded. We entered. I shouldered the door nearly closed, withholding the final pressure that would have clicked it shut.

We found ourselves in the kitchen, and from overhead I could hear the hurrying of someone small with claws.

Cheeter arrived shortly, glancing at the door.

"His workshop is downstairs," he said. "I'll show you the way."

We followed him through a door off of the kitchen, and down a creaking stairway. Below, we immediately came into a large room that smelled of the out-of-doors. Cut branches, baskets of leaves and roots, cartons of mistletoe were stacked haphazardly along the walls, on shelves, and on benches. Animal skins occupied several tabletops and were strewn over the room's three chairs. Diagrams were chalked in blue and green on both ceiling and floor, with one prominent red one covering much of the far wall. A collection of ephemeridae and of books in Gaelic and Latin filled a small bookcase beside the door.

"The sickle," I said.

Cheeter sprang atop a small table, landing amid herbs. Turning, he leaned forward, hooked his claws beneath the front edge of a small drawer. He jiggled it and drew upon it. It began to move forward to this prompting.

"Unlocked," he observed. "Let's see now."

He drew it farther open, so that, rising onto my hind legs, I could see into it. It was lined with blue velvet which bore a sickle-shaped impression at its center.

"As you can see," he stated, "it's gone."

"Anyplace else it might be?" I asked.

"No," he replied. "If it isn't here, it was with him. Those are the alternatives."

"I didn't see it anywhere out back," Graymalk said, "on the ground, or in that—mess."

"Then I'd say that someone took it," Cheeter said.

"Odd," I said then. "It was a thing of power, but not really one of the Game tools—like the wands, the icon, the pentacle, and, usually, the ring."

"Then someone just wanted it for the power, I guess," Cheeter said. "Mostly, I think, they wanted Owen out of the Game."

"Probably. I'm trying to link his death to Rastov's now. It would be strange to consider the killer as one player, though, with Owen an opener and Rastov a closer."

"Hm," Cheeter said, jumping down. "I don't know. Maybe. Maybe not. Rastov and Owen had some long talks very recently. I got the impression from listening that Owen was trying to talk Rastov into switching—all his liberal sympathies and his Russian sentiments could have been pushing him in a revolutionary direction."

"Really?" Graymalk said. "Then if someone is killing openers, Jill could be in danger. Who else might have known of their talks?"

"No one I can think of. I don't think Rastov even told Quicklime—and I didn't tell anyone, till now."

"Where did they talk?" she asked.

"Upstairs. Kitchen or parlor."

"Could anyone have been eavesdropping?"

"Only someone small enough and mobile enough to manage the squirrel hole upstairs, I suppose."

I paced slowly.

"Are Morris and MacCab openers or closers?" I asked.

"I'm pretty sure they're openers," Graymalk said.

"Yes," Cheeter agreed. "They are."

"What about the Good Doctor?"

"Nobody knows. The divinations keep going askew for him."

"The secret player," I said, "whoever it is."

"You really think there is one?" Graymalk asked.

"It's the only reason I can think of for my calculations being regularly off."

"How do we discover who it is?" she said.

"I don't know."

"And I don't care—not anymore," Cheeter said. "I just want the simple life again. The hell with all this plotting and figuring. I wasn't a volunteer. I got drafted. Get me my shadow."

"Where is it?"

"Over there."

He turned toward the big red design on the far wall.

I looked in that direction, but could not tell what it was that he was trying to indicate.

"Sorry," I said. "I don't see—"

"There," he said, "in the design—low, to the right."

Then I saw it, something I had thought simply an effect of the lighting. A squirrel-shaped shadow overlay a part of the design. Several upright, shining pieces of metal were contained by the shadow's perimeter.

"That's it?" I said.

"Yes," he replied. "It is held there by seven silver nails."

"How does one go about releasing it?" I asked.

"The nails must be drawn."

"Is there a danger to the person who would draw them?"

"I don't know. He never said."

I reared up and extended a paw. I touched the topmost nail. It was somewhat loose, and nothing unusual happened to me. So I leaned forward, seized it with my teeth and withdrew it, dropping it then to the floor.

With my paw, I tested the remaining six. Two of them were obviously loose. These I seized, one after the other, and pulled them out with my teeth. They gleamed upon the floor, real silver, and Graymalk inspected them.

"What did you feel," she asked, "as you drew them?"

"Nothing special," I said. "Do you see anything about them that I don't?"

"No. I think the power is mainly in that design. If there is to be a reaction, look to the wall for it."

I tested the remaining four. These were tighter in place than the ones I had drawn. The shadow-outline was now undulating among them.

"Have you felt anything special while I was about it, Cheeter?" I asked.

"Yes," he replied. "I felt a small tingling at each place in my body that seemed to correspond to the place in the shadow from which the nail was removed."

"Tell me if it changes," I said, and I leaned forward, took hold of another nail, and worked it back and forth with my teeth.

It took about a half-minute to loosen, and then I dropped it to the floor and tried the other three in succession. Two seemed seated fairly tightly, and one about the same as that which I had just drawn. I took hold of the looser one and worried it till it, too, came free. By then, the shadow was shrinking and expanding regularly, as if it were flapping in the third dimension of thickness with parts of it becoming imperceptible to me each time this occurred.

"The tingling is not going away," Cheeter remarked. "I'm beginning to feel it all over now."

"Any pain involved?"

"No."

I poked with my paw at the two remaining nails. Tight. Perhaps it would be better to fetch Larry and a pair of pliers than to risk breaking my teeth on them. Still, it wouldn't hurt to try a bit first. I worried one for the better part of a minute, and it did seem to loosen slightly near the end. I stopped to rest my jaws then, promising myself I would have a go at both nails before I considered quitting.

I gave the second one—which was located about ten inches to the left of the first—well over a minute of the same treatment, and I found it hard to tell when I'd let up whether I'd affected it much.

I did not like the taste of the plaster and the pigment used in the design. I was not sure what lay beneath the plaster, holding the nails in place. Not enough of that covering had chipped away for me to distinguish the surface it covered—only enough for grit with a damp basement taste to come into my mouth.

I stepped back. The design looked slobbered-upon, and I wondered how dog spit would affect its subtle functions.

"Please don't quit," Cheeter said. "Try again."

"I'm just catching my breath," I told him. "I've been using my front teeth so far, because it was easier. I'm going to switch to the side now."

So I leaned again and took a grip with my back teeth, right side, upon the nail which seemed to have responded slightly to my suasions. I had it moving, then loosening, before too long.

Finally, I dropped it and listened. Silver makes a pleasant sound when it's struck.

"Six," I announced. "How does it feel now?"

"More tingling," Cheeter said. "Maybe some sort of anticipation."

"Last chance to quit while you're ahead," I said, as I repositioned myself to use the left side of my jaws on the final one.

"Go ahead," he told me.

So I caught hold and began to work it, slowly, with steady pressure rather than jerking movements, which I had learned from the previous one to be more effective. I feared for my teeth, but nothing cracked or chipped. As much as I liked the sound of silver, I did not like its cold metallic taste.

And all this while the shadow itself flowed over my face intermittently, passing before my eyes like a quick cloud before the sun, wrapping me momentarily, falling loose again.

I felt the nail move. My jaws were beginning to ache by then, though, and I switched sides. I've cracked large bones with my teeth, and I know the power that is there. But this required more than simple biting ability. It was the movement that was really important, involving my neck muscles as well as my jaws. Forward, back. . . .

And then the nail began to loosen. I paused to rest.

"What do we do when it's free?" I asked them. "What's to prevent its simply slipping away? Is there any special means of reattaching it?"

"I don't know," Cheeter said. "I never thought of that."

"How was it separated from you in the first place?" Graymalk asked.

"He made a light and cast it there upon the wall," Cheeter said. "He drove in the nails, then passed his sickle close to my body, somehow severing it. When I moved away, it remained. I felt different immediately."

"It will respond to your life," Graymalk said, "if you position yourself correctly and it flows over you. But your life must be exposed at the seven points which held it—and it will respond to the nails which bound it."

"What do you mean?" Cheeter asked.

"Blood," she said. "You must scratch a wound on the back of each paw, one atop your head, one at the middle of your tail, one midback—the seven places the shadow was pierced. When Snuff removes the final nail he must take care not simply to draw it straight out but to drag it downward, snagging the shadow, pulling it to cover you. You will then be standing with a foot on each of the four nails which held the paws, your tail resting upon that of the tail, your head extended and down to touch the sixth—"

"I don't know which nail is which now," he said.

"I do," she replied. "I've been watching. Then Snuff will drag the shadow over you and drop its nail upon your back at the place of the seventh wound. This should serve to bind it to you again."

"Gray," I said, "how do you know all this?"

"I was recently given a small wisdom," she responded.

"By the high cat—"

"Hush!" she said. "This place is not that place. Leave it there."

"Sorry."

She moved to position the nails, and Cheeter scratched himself—paws, head, and tail. I could smell his blood.

"I can't reach my back for the seventh," he said.

Her right paw slashed forward, opening a bright inch at the the middle of his back. It came too fast for him even to flinch.

"There," she said. "Position yourself upon the nails now, as I have instructed."

He moved and did so, sprawled motionless then.

I returned to the final nail, taking hold and pulling slowly. As soon as I felt it come loose I dragged it down the wall and across the floor toward Cheeter, never lifting it from contact with a surface the entire while. I had no idea, though, whether the shadow was coming along with it, and I was in no position to ask. Still, if it weren't, I guessed Graymalk would have said something.

"Lead it over him and drop it upon his back," she said, "at the place of my mark."

I did that, stepping back immediately afterwards.

"Do you know whether it's taken hold?" I asked Cheeter.

"I can't tell," he said.

"Do you feel any different?"

"I don't know."

"What now, Gray?" I asked. "How long do we wait to see whether it's attached?"

"Let's give it a minute or two," she replied.

"The design," Cheeter said then. "It's changing."

I turned and looked. There might have been a trace of movement to it as I did so, but it was gone by the time I faced it. It did look smaller, though, a bit less extended to the left, and differently disposed to the right. And its colors seemed brighter.

"I think that means it's in place now," he said. "I want to move."

He sprang up and raced across the floor, scattering the nails. He bounded halfway up the stair, turned, and looked back at us. It was too dim to see whether he'd achieved the desired result.

"Come on!" he said. "Let's go out!"

We followed him, and I opened the kitchen door without difficulty. As soon as I did, he rushed past us.

The sun had come out, and as he flashed across the yard we could see the shadow which accompanied him. He leaped up onto the wall, hesitated, looked back.

"Thanks!" he said.

"Where are you headed?" I asked.

"The woods," he answered. "Good-bye."

Then he was off the wall and away.

October 26

I T WAS A SLOW DAY. NO ROUNDS TO MAKE. Just an occasional glance at the bottle of port, which had begun glowing faintly. I took several walks and visited briefly with Graymalk. She had nothing new to report. Strolled around Rastov's place, but Quicklime was nowhere in sight. Sniffed about Morris and MacCab's, but Nightwind had retired somewhere for the day. Walked up to Larry's, to keep him current on events, but he was out. Wandered over to the Good Doctor's storm-crowned quarters, but there was no activity there that was viewable from without. Made my way to the Great Detective's domicile, but all was quiet at the manse. I couldn't really tell whether he was there or not. Passed the church and the vicarage a couple of times, and Tekela saw me the second time by and flew away. Went back home and ate. Took a nap.

I grew restless in the evening and went out again. Graymalk wasn't out and Larry wasn't back. I ran

across a field and then decided to prowl the woods, to keep the old instincts in shape. Frightened a few rabbits. Sniffed out a fox's trail and tracked it for a time. Clever little lady, though. She picked up on me, doubled back, and lost me in a stream. Good to be reminded of these matters.

Suddenly, I decided to take a hint and enter the stream myself. Upstream was downwind, so I headed that way, which is what the fox had probably done, too, when she'd realized what I was just then realizing, about being followed.

My tracker was pretty clumsy, though, and it was not difficult to make my way back, staying downwind and keeping to cover, and to surprise him there at the stream's edge.

He was big, bigger than me, wolf-sized.

"Larry?" I called. "I've been looking for you."

"Yes?" came the reply.

"You're not Larry," I said.

"No."

"Why were you following me?"

"I just wandered by a few days ago, and I was thinking of spending the winter in this wood. This is a very strange place, though. The people in the area do peculiar things—often to each other. I followed you when I saw you, to ask how safe it might be for me."

"Some of them are getting ready for something that will be happening at the end of the month," I said. "Lie low till it's past and you'll probably be all right for the winter, if you exercise a little discretion when you take a sheep or a pig. Don't leave carcasses in plain sight, I mean."

"What's going on at the end of the month?"

"Weird stuff," I said. "A little specialized craziness. Stay away from any human gatherings that night."

"Why?"

About then, a little moonlight reached us through the branches.

"Because it might get you killed—or worse."

"I don't understand."

"You don't have to," I said, and I turned and got out.

"Snuff! Wait! Come back!" he called.

But I just kept going. He tried to follow me, but Growler'd shown me stuff that even the fox would have been proud of. I lost him easily.

In the moonlight I'd recognized him from his likeness in the ward-screen as one of the prowlers who'd been snooping around while we were in London. Maybe he'd just been checking things out, as he'd said. But put that together with his knowing my name when I hadn't given it to him, and I didn't like it a bit.

Overhead, growing in strength, the older, wiser moon paced me. I'd give her a run for her silver.

October 27

I WAS AWAKENED BY A SCRATCHING ON THE back door. I went to it and pushed my hatch open. Graymalk was sitting before it, waiting. It occurred to me that I can't tell when she's smiling either.

I checked the sky, which was cloudy with blue breaks.

"Good morning," I said then.

" 'Morning, Snuff. Did I wake you?"

I stepped outside and stretched.

"Yes," I said. "But I was oversleeping. Thanks."

"How are your aches and pains?"

"Much improved. Your own?"

"Better."

"Yesterday was pretty quiet," I said, "for a change."

"But last night was a different matter," she said.

"Oh? What do you mean?"

"Then you haven't heard about the fire?"

"Fire? No. Where? What happened?"

"The Good Doctor got burned out. It's still smoldering. I took a walk very early this morning and I smelled it. Went over and watched for a long time. His storm finally stopped when the place caved in."

"Is he all right? And the other fellows? Did they get out?"

"I don't know. I'm not sure they did, though. I didn't see them."

"Maybe I ought to sniff around a bit," I said.

"Might be a good idea."

We headed off in that direction.

It was odd, coming on the place without a storm raging overhead. The house was blackened and still smoky, its roof and three walls fallen, the ground dark with ashes, débris, and the singeing effects of the heat, about it. Off to the west—to our right, as we approached—the barn stood unscathed. The ground everywhere near us was wet to the point of squishiness from the deluge that had descended upon it in past weeks.

We circled the burnt place slowly, peering into it. Past charred beams and fragmented walls, I could make out banks of broken equipment far below. The smell from the fire and the dampness of the earth made it impossible for me to detect any useful scents in the vicinity. I told Graymalk this, and she said, "Then you can't tell whether the Good Doctor and his assistants escaped or perished?"

"Afraid not," I answered.

We went off to take a look at the barn. As we departed the ravaged area and neared that structure,

I did pick up a fresh scent. Very fresh. Just ahead, in fact. I broke into a run.

"What is it?" Graymalk asked.

There was no time to respond to her. I'd glimpsed him rounding the corner of the building, and I raced that way. He saw me coming, realized that I could move a lot faster than he could, and dashed inside one of a number of wooden crates strewn there. I approached the crate and stuck my head inside, fangs bared.

Bubo crouched in its farthest recess.

"Remember what they say about cornered rats," he said. "We can be nasty."

"I'm sure," I replied. "But what'd be the point? No one wants to hurt you."

"You were chasing me."

"I wanted to talk to you."

"So you brought along a cat."

"I can let you talk to her if you don't want to talk to me."

I started to withdraw.

"No! Wait! I'd rather talk to you!"

"All right," I said. "I just wanted to know what happened here."

"There was a fire."

"I can see that. How'd it get started?"

"The experiment man got mad at the Good Doctor and started wrecking the lab. Sparks from some of the equipment set the place burning."

" 'The experiment man'?"

"You know. The big fellow the Good Doctor put together from all the parts his assistant dug up for him."

I recalled the smell of death and I began to understand.

"What happened then?" I asked.

"The experiment man ran out and hid in the barn here, as he always did after an argument. I got out, too. The place burned down."

"Did the Good Doctor and his assistant get out in time?"

"I don't know. When I went back and looked later there was no way I could tell."

"What about the experiment man? Is he still in the barn?"

"No. He ran away later. I don't know where he is."

I backed up. "I'm sorry," I said, and I withdrew my head from the crate.

Graymalk immediately moved near and asked, "Was the Good Doctor an opener or a closer?"

"Please," he said, "let me be. I'm just a simple pack rat. Snuff! Don't let her have me!"

"I've already eaten," she said. "Besides, I owe you courtesy as a fellow player."

"No you don't," he said. "It's over. Over."

"Just because your master is dead doesn't mean I should treat you as anything other than a player."

"But you know. You must know. You're toying with me. Cats are that way. I'm not a player. I never was. Have you really eaten recently?"

"Yes."

"That's worse then. You'll toy more."

"Shut up a minute!" she said.

"See? There goes the courtesy."

"Be still. I *am* starting to get angry. What do you mean you were never a player?"

"Just that. I saw a good thing and I decided to jump aboard."

"You'd better explain."

"I told you I was just a pack rat. I used to hear all you folks talking—Nightwind, Quicklime, Cheeter, you and Snuff—as I lurked about my business. I got the idea pretty quick that there was some sort of strange Game going on, and you were all players. You all had it pretty good and you all left each other alone, even helped each other sometimes. So I decided to learn as much about your Game as I could and figure out how I could pass for one of you. I realized pretty quickly that you all had pretty weird masters and mistresses. Then I knew that I could do it. After all, I'd been hanging around the Good Doctor's place already, for the leftovers from his work. So I let on that he was in the Game and that I worked for him. Sure enough, I got respect and decent treatment from the rest of you. It made life a lot easier. What a tragedy—the fire. It'll be rough spending winter in the barn. But rats are adaptable. We—"

"Be still," she said again, and he obeyed. "Snuff, do you realize what this means?"

"Yes," I said. "There was no secret player. What it was, was that I had one player too many in my calculations. The Good Doctor must just have come here seeking a little privacy for his work."

". . . And that explains why the divinations concerning him were always ambiguous."

"Of course. I'll have to do some new figuring, soon. —Thank you, Bubo. You've just helped me quite a bit."

Graymalk moved away from the crate and Bubo peered out.

"You mean I can go?" he said.

I was feeling generous, happy even, at the final piece for my puzzle. And he looked kind of pathetic.

"Or you can come with us, if you like," I said. "You don't have to live in the barn. You can stay at my place. It's warm and there's plenty to eat."

"You really mean that?"

"Sure. You've been a help."

"Of course you do live near a cat. . . ."

Graymalk made her laughing sound.

"You gave us professional help," she said. "I'll leave you on my professional courtesy list."

"All right, I'll do it," he told me.

He emerged and we headed back.

October 28

I KNEW, BUT OF COURSE I HAD TO CHECK IT out by laying it on the terrain. I strolled by most of the places I had visited yesterday, wondering who else might have figured it out yet. I saw the vicar and he saw me, from a distance, after Tekela'd brought her notice of me to his attention, in passing. He was just carrying a carton into the vicarage from a wagon, and he stopped to glare. He was still wearing the bandage on his ear. The Great Detective Mrs. Enderby happened to be in a tree in her yard with a pair of binoculars when I passed, and called out to me.

"Snuff, please come here!"

I kept going.

The sun was shining intermittently through masses of clouds. Yet more leaves, fallen and falling, were scudding in the breezes. I headed south.

Bubo had set up housekeeping in our basement,

though he wandered the house with our leave and ate with me in the kitchen.

"What became of the Things in the Mirror? Or to the mirror, for that matter?" he'd asked.

So I told him the story of the attack, following our trip to town. Which led into the story of our trip to town.

"Wouldn't put it past the vicar," he said. "He's taken many a shot at me with that crossbow of his, and I never did anything to him, except hunt through his dustbin on occasion. Is that cause to put an arrow in a fellow? I hope he fudges the final business and you fellows blow him to oblivion."

"Just how much do you know about the Game, anyway?" I asked.

"I've heard a lot. I've seen a lot. Everybody talked freely because they assumed I was a part of it. After a time, I almost got to feeling I was," he reflected. "I know so much about it."

And he proceeded to tell me the story of how a number of the proper people are attracted to the proper place in the proper year on a night in the lonesome October when the moon shines full on Halloween and the way may be opened for the return of the Elder Gods to Earth, and of how some of these people would assist in the opening of the way for them while others would strive to keep the way closed. For ages, the closers have won—often just barely—and there were stories of a shadowy man, half-mad, a killer, a wanderer, and his dog, who always showed up to attempt the closing. Some said that he was Cain himself, doomed to walk the Earth, marked; others said he'd a pact with one of the Elders who secretly wished to thwart the others; none really knew. And the people would acquire certain tools and other objects of power, meet together at the designated spot and attempt to work their wills. The winners walked away, the losers suffered for their presumption by a reaction from the cosmic principles involved in the attempt. Then he named the players and their tools, adding an awareness of the calculation, of divinations, of magical attacks and defenses.

"Bubo," I said, "you have impressed me as few have impressed me—learning all that without giving yourself away."

"Rats have strong survival instincts," he said. "I needed to know it to stay safe in this area."

"No, you didn't," I said. "You could have remained out of it and gone about your business. The deception itself was a lot more dangerous."

"All right. I got curious about all these cryptic comments I kept hearing. Probably too curious for my own good. What it was, I think, is that I enjoyed pretending I was playing, too. I'd never done anything important before, and it felt good."

"Come on," I told him. "Get up on my back, and I'll take you to see the Gipsies. Good music and all."

We stayed late at the camp. I don't have that many friends, and it was a good evening.

As I made my way to Dog's Nest I came across another set of the huge, misshapen footprints at the hill's base. There were some up on top, too. I wondered where the experiment man would go, now his home was destroyed.

I made a circuit of the hilltop, drawing my lines again, laying them out upon the land, excluding the ruined farmhouse to the southwest now, which moved things considerably northward, taking into account the two satellite graves, trying it both with and without Larry's place in the formulation. With it, it came to another nothing wilderness spot. Without it, however, came a place already touched by the High Powers. I was standing upon it. It was here, Dog's Nest, amid its broken circle of stone, where the final act would take place. Larry was just a friend of the court. I threw back my head and howled. The design was complete.

On the rock where our earlier adventure had begun the inscription flared briefly, as if in endorsement.

I departed quickly, skipping upon the hill.

Midnight.

"I've found it, Jack!" I said, and I told him Bubo's story.

". . . And subtracting the Good Doctor leaves us atop my hill," I concluded.

"Of course the others will divine it within the next few days."

". . . And the word will be passed. True. I can only recall one time when no one figured it properly."

"My, that was long ago. . . ."

"Yes, and we all sat down to dinner together, made a joke of it, and went our ways."

"Such things are rare."

"Indeed."

"I think this will be a close one, Snuff."

"So do I. And it's been a strange one from the start. This quality may carry through."

"Oh?"

"Just a feeling."

"I trust your instincts. We must be ready for anything. Too bad about Jill and Graymalk."

"I've decided I will stay friends with them to the end," I said.

He squeezed my shoulder.

"As you would."

"It's *not* like Dijon, is it?" I asked.

"No. Many odd things have happened this time around," he said. "Stiff upper lip, friend."

"That's how I smile," I said.

October 29

FOLLOWING LUNCH AT JILL'S PLACE—TO which Bubo was also invited, having finally acknowledged Graymalk to be a cat of a different category—I took a walk back to the ruin of the Good Doctor's place. The meal had had an almost elegiac quality to it, Jack having asked outright whether she'd consider switching, Jill having admitted to a conflict in her sympathies now, but being determined to play the Game through as she'd started. It felt odd to be dining with the enemy and to care that much about them. So I took a walk afterwards, more for something to do while being alone than for any pressing purpose.

I took my time in going. The charred ruin still smelled strongly; and though I circled it many times, I could see no bones or other signs of dead humans within. I wandered over to the barn then, wondering whether the experiment man might have returned to it to hide.

The door was opened sufficiently for me to enter, and I did. While his disconcerting odor was present, it did not seem a recent thing, as smells went. Still, I sought in each stall, even stirring through the hay. I checked in every corner, cubby, and bin. I even mounted the ladder to the loft and looked about there.

Then I noticed a peculiar shape to the rear—that of a bat hanging from a beam. While all bats look pretty much alike to me, especially when you turn them upside-down, it reminded me a lot of Needle. I approached and said loudly, "Hey, Needle! What the hell are you doing here?"

It stirred slightly, but did not seem inclined to wake up. So I reached out and prodded it with my paw.

"Come on, Needle. I want to talk to you," I said.

It unfurled its wings and stared at me. It yawned, then, "Snuff, what are you doing here?" it said.

"Checking out the aftermath of the fire. What about you?"

"Same thing, but daylight caught me and I decided to sleep here."

"Does the experiment man still come here?"

"I don't know. He hasn't today. And I don't know whether the Good Doctor got away either. How's the Game progressing?"

"Now I've learned that the Good Doctor was never in it, I've found the point of manifestation—the big hill with the fallen stones."

"Really. Now that's interesting. What else is new?"

"Rastov and Owen are dead. Quicklime and Cheeter went back to the woods."

"Yes, I'd heard that."

"So it seems someone's killing openers."

"Rastov was a closer."

"I think Owen talked him into switching."

"No, he tried but he didn't succeed."

"How do you know that?"

"I used to get into Owen's place through Cheeter's attic hole and listen to them talk. I was there the night before Rastov was killed. They were drinking and quoting everybody from Thomas Paine to Nietzsche at each other, but Rastov didn't switch."

"Interesting. You sound as if you're still in the Game."

There came a faint sound from below, just as he said, "Oh, I am— Get down! Flat!"

I threw myself onto my right side. A crossbow bolt passed very near and embedded itself into the wall right above me. I turned my head and saw Vicar Roberts below, near to the door, just lowering the weapon. His face held a nasty smile.

If I ran and jumped I'd be downstairs in a trice. I might also break a leg in the process, though, and then he could finish me easily. The alternative was to climb down the way I'd come up, backing down the ladder. For anatomical reasons, my descent is always slower than my ascent. If I did not do this, however, he could crank the weapon back, seat a bolt, and come up after me. In that case, the odds would be in his favor. At least, he didn't have any armed assistants with him. . . .

I thought back quickly, recalling how long it usually took to get such a weapon cocked. There was no choice, and there was no time to wait if I were to have any chance at all.

I rushed to the head of the ladder, turned, and began my descent. The vicar had already lowered the bow by then and commenced rearming it. I moved as fast as I was able, but as I searched with a hind leg after each wooden crosspiece my back felt terribly exposed. Should I make it to the floor unpierced I knew that I would still be at high risk. I hurried. I saw something black flutter by.

I heard the final click. I heard the sounds of his fitting the quarrel into place. It was still a good distance down. I descended another step. I imagined him raising the weapon, taking a leisurely sighting at an easy target. I hoped that I was right about the fluttering, about Needle. Another step. . . .

I knew that I was right when I heard the vicar utter an oath. I descended one more step. . . . Then I decided I could risk no more. I pushed myself backward, letting myself fall the rest of the way, recalling things Graymalk had said about always landing on her feet, wishing I'd been born with that ability, trying to achieve it this one time, anyway. . . .

I tried to torque my body in the proper direction— along the long axis, relaxing my legs the while. The bolt passed well above me, from the sound I heard of it striking wood. But the man was already cranking the weapon again as I hit the ground. I did land on my feet, but they went out from under me immediately. As I struggled to rise, I saw him finish cocking the thing, now ignoring the black form which darted before him. My left hind leg hurt. I pushed myself upright, anyway, and turned. He had the quarrel in one hand and was moving to fit it into place. I had to rush him, to try knocking him over before he succeeded and got off another shot. I knew that it was going to be close. . . .

And then there was a shadow in the doorway at his back.

"Why, Vicar Roberts, whatever are you doing with that archaic weapon?" came the wonderfully controlled falsetto of the Great Detective in his Linda Enderby guise.

The vicar hesitated, then turned.

"Madam," he said, "I was about to perform a community service by dispatching a vicious brute which even now is preparing to attack us."

I began wagging my tail immediately and put on my idiot slobbering hound expression, tongue hanging out and all.

"That hardly seems a vicious beast to me," the voice of the lady stated, as the Great Detective moved in quickly, passing between the vicar and myself to effectively block a shot. "That's just old Snuff. Everybody knows Snuff. Not a mean bone in his body. Good Snuff! Good dog!"

The old hand-on-head business followed, patting. I responded as if it were the greatest invention since free lunch.

"Whatever made you think him antisocial?"

"Madam, that was the creature that almost tore my ear off."

"I am certain you must be mistaken, sir. I cannot conceive of this animal as behaving aggressively—except possibly in self-defense."

The vicar's face was quite red and his shoulders looked very tense. For a moment I thought he might actually try angling in a shot at me, anyhow.

"I really feel," the Linda voice went on, "that if you have any complaints concerning the animal you ought to take them up with his owner first before embarking on a drastic action that might well draw the attention of the Humane Society and not rest well with the parishioners."

"That man is a godless jackanapes . . ." he began, but then his shoulders slumped. "Perhaps, however, I acted hastily. As you say, the parishioners might view it askance, not knowing the full measure of my complaints. Yes. Very well." He lowered the weapon and released its tension. "This will be settled," he said then, "in another day or two. But for now I accept your counsel and will do nothing rash." He put away the quarrel in a case slung over his shoulder, slinging the weapon, also, moments later. "And so, madam, I thank you again for those cookies you brought by, which I found quite tasty, and I bid you a good day."

"I trust your daughter enjoyed them as well?"

"Indeed she did. We both thank you."

He turned then and passed out through the door. The Great Detective immediately followed him to it and peered out, doubtless to make certain that he was indeed departing. Before I could take the same route to the same end, however, he caught hold of the door and slid it the rest of the way shut.

Turning, he studied me.

"Snuff," he said, the falsetto vanished, "you are fortunate that I have a good pair of binoculars and have been inclined to use them of late.

"You are a very unusual creature," he continued. "I first encountered you in Soho when assisting some friends at the Yard in their investigation of a very unusual series of killings. Subsequently, I have found you to be present in numerous situations both bizarre and intriguing. Your presence seems to have become almost a common denominator to all of the recent peculiar occurrences in this area. It long ago passed the point where I could safely deem it a matter of coincidence."

I sat down and scratched my left ear with my hind leg.

"That is not going to work with me, Snuff," he said. "I know that you are not just a dumb dog, a subhuman intelligence. I have learned a great deal concerning the affairs of this month, this place, the people engaged in the enterprise which I believe you refer to as 'the Game.'"

I paused in my scratching to study his face.

"I interviewed both the inebriated Russian and the equally distracted Welshman on their ways home from the pub one night, in my guise as a jovial traveler in commercial sales. I have spoken with the Gipsies, with your neighbors, with all of the principals involved in this matter of purported metaphysical conflict—yes, I know it to be that—and I have observed many things which permitted me to deduce the outlines of a dark picture."

I yawned in the rude way dogs sometimes do. He smiled.

"No good, Snuff," he said. "You can dispense with the mannerisms. I am certain that you understand every word I am saying, and you must be curious as to the extent of my knowledge of the ceremony to be conducted here on All Hallows' Eve and my intentions concerning it."

He paused, and we studied each other. He wasn't giving anything away, even at the olfactory level.

"So I think it is time for a sign of good faith," he finally said. "Apart from the fact that I may just have rescued you from mortal distress, there are more things that I wish to say and some that I need to know, and I believe these would benefit you as well as myself. If you would be so good as to acknowledge my words, I will proceed."

I looked away. I had anticipated this as soon as he had begun addressing me in a rational fashion. I still had not decided what my response should be when he finally got around to asking for what had to be a token of faith. And that is what it came down to . . . faith in the man's professional integrity, though I was certain he would not approve of the goings-on here, and I'd no idea where his significant loyalty lay—to law, or to justice; nor whether he really understood what was at stake. Still, I did want to know what he had learned and what he had intended, and I knew there would be no way for him later to prove his assumptions concerning myself even if I did give him the acknowledgment he wanted.

So I looked back at him, met his eyes for several long seconds, then nodded once.

"Very good," he responded. "To continue: A great number of crimes have apparently been committed by nearly everyone involved in this 'Game,' as you call it. Many of them would be virtually impossible to demonstrate in court—but I have neither a client who requires that I find a way of doing so, nor inclination to pursue such matters for my own amusement. Technically, I am here only as a friend of the Yard,

for purposes of investigating the likely murder of a
police officer. And this matter will be dealt with in
due time. Since my arrival in this place, however, I
have been more and more impressed by the unusual
goings-on, until, at length—largely because of Mr.
Talbot's strange condition and that of the one known
as the Count—I have become convinced that there
is something truly unnatural involved. While I dislike
such a conclusion, recent personal experiences have
also led me to accept its validity. Such being the case,
I am moved to interfere with your 'Game' two days
hence."

I shook my head slowly, from side to side.

"Snuff, that rascal who just left is planning to
murder his stepdaughter on All Hallows' Eve!"

I nodded.

"You countenance this behavior?"

I shook my head from side to side, then turned
and walked away from him to a place where dust lay
heavy upon the floorboards. With my paw I made
four strokes in the dust: LT.

He followed me and watched. Then he said slowly,
"Lawrence Talbot?"

I nodded.

"He plans to prevent the killing?"

I nodded again.

"Snuff, I know more about him than he realizes,
and I have experimented with many sorts of drugs
myself over the years. I know that his intent is to
rescue Lynette on the night of the ceremony, but I do
not believe that he has sufficiently refined the dosage
which he feels will carry him past the moon madness
of his affliction. And whatever the case, Vicar Roberts

is aware that there is one of his sort involved, and he has melted down a piece of the rectory silverware to cast a bullet for a pistol he will be carrying with him that night."

He paused and studied me. I believed him, but I did not know what to do.

"The only part I can see for myself in this entire affair would be to effect the girl's rescue, should Mr. Talbot fail. To do this, I require something from you: I must know where the ceremony is to take place. Do you know?"

I nodded.

"Will you show me?"

I nodded again, and I looked toward the door.

For a second his hand twitched toward my head, then he lowered it and smiled. He moved to the door and slid it open. We stepped outside, where I looked in the direction of Dog's Nest and barked once. Then I began walking. He followed.

October 30

HERE WAS NOT A GREAT DEAL TO DO TODAY. And tomorrow will likely be the same. Till night. Those of us who remain will gather atop the hill at midnight. We will bring kindling, and we will cooperate in the building of a big fire. It will serve as illumination, and into it will be cast all the bones, herbs, and other ingredients we have been preparing all month to give ourselves an edge and to confound our enemies. It may stink. It may smell wonderful. Forces will wrestle within it, play about it, giving to it a multicolored nimbus, and occasionally causing it to produce musical sounds and wailings amid its crackling and popping. Then we will position ourselves in an arc before the thing our divinations have shown us to be the Gateway—which we have already determined to be the stone bearing the inscription. The openers and their friends will

stand at one end of the arc, the closers at the other. All will have brought the tools they intend to employ. Some of these are neutral, such as the ring, the pentacle, the icon, to take their character— of opening, or closing—from the hands of those who wield them; others—the two wands, one for opening, one for closing—will naturally be held by those of these persuasions. Jill holds the Opening Wand, my master the Closing Wand. The forces of the neutral objects will support the efforts of that side for which they are employed, which makes the outcome sound like a simple mathematical affair. But it isn't. The strength of the individual counts for much; and these affairs seem to generate strange byplay as well, which contributes to overall dispositions of power. And then there is the matter of experience. Theoretically, everything should be conducted at a metaphysical level, but this is seldom really the case. Still, no matter how physical it may get, the reputation attached to Jack and his knife generally grants us considerable protection against mundane violence. We tend to maintain our positions in the arc once the ceremony has begun, and sometimes things happen to players during its course. There is a sort of psychic circuit established among us. It need not be disastrous to break the arc, though it may be a courting of mischance somewhere along the line. Preliminary rites will begin, as a matter of individual choice, often at odds with one another. The power will build and build. To back it in its shifting, psychic attacks may be shot back and forth. Disasters may follow. Players may fall, or go mad, catch fire, be transformed. The Gateway may begin to open at any time, or it may await the invitation of the Opening Wand. The resistance will begin immediately. The Closing Wand will be employed, and any ancillary forces that may feed it. Eventually, at the end of our exercises—which may take only a little while, though conceivably they could last until dawn (and in such a stalemated case, the closers would win by default)— the matter will be decided. Bad things happen to the losers.

But one thing remained undone. I headed up the road. I had to find Larry. I had delayed too long in telling him the truth about Linda Enderby. Now I also had to tell him what the vicar had divined, and about the silver bullet that awaited him. This could call for a radical revision of his plan.

I barked and scratched at his door several times. There was no answer. I circled the place, peering in windows, scratching, barking repeatedly. No response. It seemed deserted.

Rather than depart, however, I circled again, sniffing, analyzing every scent. His was strongest to the rear of the house, indication of his most recent departure. Nose low then, I followed the trail he had left. It led back to a small grove of trees at the rear of his property. I could hear a faint sound of running water from within the grove.

Making my way through it, I discovered that the small stream which traversed his property had here been diverted to the extent of filling a little pool before it departed. Small, humped bridges crossed the stream—both the entering flow and the departing one. The ground had been cleared for some distance on both sides of it and covered with a layer of sand. A number of fairly large, mossy rocks were artfully disposed, yet in an almost casual-seeming fashion. The sand was raked in swirling patterns. A few low plants grew here and there about the area.

Beside the largest of the rocks, facing east, Larry sat in a meditative posture, his eyes more than half-closed, his breathing barely discernible.

I was loath to disturb his meditation or the peace of the place, and had I known how long he might be about it, I would have been willing to wait, or even to go away and return later. But there was no way for me to tell, and since the news I brought him involved the safety of his life, I approached him.

"Larry," I said. "It's me, Snuff. Hate to bother you. . . ."

But I hadn't. He gave no sign of having heard me.

I repeated what I had said, studying his face, his breathing. There were no changes in either.

I reached out and touched him with my paw. No reaction.

I barked loudly, several times. It was as if I hadn't. He had gone pretty far, wherever it was that he had gone.

So I threw back my head and howled. He didn't notice, and it didn't matter that he didn't notice. It's a good thing to do when you're frustrated.

October 31

AND SO THE DAY ARRIVED, CLOUDY, AND WITH a small wind out of the north. I told myself that I was not nervous, that as an old hand at this there were no jitters of anticipation, rushes of anxiety, waves of pure fear. But I had gone down to the basement to begin my rounds when I realized that there were no rounds to make, and I found myself returning to check our assembly of ingredients and tools over and over again.

Finally, I went out and visited Larry's place. He was gone from his grove and the house seemed empty.

I went looking for Graymalk, and when we met we took a walk together.

We hiked for a long time in silence before she said, "You and Jack will be the only closers there."

"It looks that way," I said.

"I'm sorry."

"That's okay."

"Jill and I will be going to a meeting at the vicarage this afternoon. Morris and MacCab will be there, too."

"Oh? Strategy session?"

"I guess so."

We climbed to Dog's Nest and looked around. An altarlike raised area of boulders had been built up before the big stone. Heavy boards lay across it. Some kindling for the banefire was already stacked, farther off.

"Right there," she said.

"Yes."

"We're going to protest the sacrifice part."

"Good."

"You think Larry will be able to do what he plans?"

"I don't know."

We climbed down a different way than we'd gone up, discovering some fresh misshapen footprints.

"I wonder what'll become of the big fellow now," she said. "I feel sorry for him. That night he picked me up he didn't mean to hurt me, I could tell."

"Another lost one," I said. "Yes, sad."

We walked again in silence, then, "I want to stand near you in the arc," she said. "I believe the vicar will be at the left end, with Morris and MacCab next to him, Tekela and Nightwind with them, then Jill. I will stand to her right. I will assume a position three paces forward. That would put you and Jack beside us."

"Oh?"

"Yes, I've been working for this arrangement. You must be to my right and slightly back—that is, to Jack's left."

"Why?"

"Because something bad may happen if you stand to his right."

"How do you know this?"

"My small wisdom."

I thought about it. The old cat in the Dreamworld was obviously on her side, and she was an opener. Therefore, he could be setting me up for something. However, his remarks concerning the Elders had almost seemed disparaging, and he had seemed kindly disposed toward me. Reason stopped here. I knew that I had to trust my feelings.

"I'll do it."

When we neared our area, I said, "I'm going to walk over again to see whether Larry's back. Want to come with?"

"No. That meeting. . . ."

"All right. Well—It's—been good."

"Yes. I never knew a dog this well before."

"Same with cats and me. I'll see you later, then."

"Yes."

She headed home.

I searched all around Larry's place again, but there was no sign of his return.

On my way home, I heard my name hissed from a clump of weeds.

"Snuff, old boy. Good to see you. I was on my way over. Saved me a trip. . . ."

"Quicklime! What have you been up to?"

"Hanging out in that orchard, eating the hard stuff," he said. "Just stopped by for a quick one, on the way over."

"Why were you coming to see me?"

"Learned something. Wanted you to know."

"What?" I asked.

"I picked up a bad habit from Rastov, I guess. Look at me. I feel like I'm shedding my skin."

"You're not."

"I know. But I really liked him. When I left you, I headed for the orchard and just started eating the old, fermented ones. It was—snug—with him. I felt like somebody needed me. The fruit's almost gone now. I'll come around. I'll be all right. But I'll miss him. He was a good man. The vicar got him—that's what Nightwind told me. Wanted to narrow the field. That's why the Count disposed of Owen—to send the vicar a message. You'll get the vicar, won't you?"

"Quick, I think you've had too much. Owen was killed after the Count was staked."

"Clever, isn't he? That's what I was coming to tell you about. He fooled us. He's still around."

"What? How?"

"When I reached the peak of my indulgence the other night," he replied, "I suddenly felt terribly lonely. I didn't want to be alone, so I went looking for someone, something—lights, movement, sounds. I went over to the Gipsy camp, which was perfect. I curled up beneath a wagon, planning to spend the night there and sleep it off. But I overheard parts of a conversation from the wagon which led me to make my way up between its floorboards. I had chosen *the* wagon, and a pair of guards were in it. Sometimes they'd speak in their own tongue, sometimes in English—the younger one wanted the practice. I spent the night in there instead of below. But I learned the story. I even found an opening that gave me a view of the casket.

"He's with the Gipsies?"

"Yes. They guard him by day as he sleeps, guard the casket at night when he's away."

"So he'd faked it," I said. "Dressed the skeleton we'd found in his garments, put the stake into it himself."

"Yes, the crumbly skeleton that was already there."

". . . And that's why the ring wasn't on it."

"Yes, and he was safe in that, too. Anybody finding the remains would assume that the staker had taken it."

I felt a chill.

"Quick, he did make this arrangement after the death of the moon, didn't he?"

"Yes. Your calculations would be unaffected."

"Good. But this I don't understand—the Count killed Owen because the vicar killed Rastov. Owen was an opener. Does that reflect a particular sympathy on the part of the Count? Or was he simply out to check the vicar and keep the violence from spreading?"

"I don't know. Nothing was said on the matter."

I growled softly.

"This is a complicated one," I said.

"Agreed. Now you know everything I do."

"Thanks. Want to come with me?"

"No. I'm really out of the Game. Good luck."

" 'Luck, Quick."

I heard him slither off.

It rained a little that afternoon, and stopped shortly after sunset. I went outside to look for the moon, and Bubo came with me. The clouds still veiled her, however, and all we could see was the big area of brightness she shed in the east. The wind blew chill.

"So this is it," Bubo said. "By morning it will all be decided."

"Yes."

"I wish I could have been playing all along."

"A wish on the moon," I said. "It may be true. You have been playing, in a way. You've traded information, you've watched things develop, same as the rest of us."

"Yes, but I didn't really *do* important things like the rest of you."

"It's mainly the little things—all added up—that give us the final picture, that make the difference."

"I suppose so," he said. "Yes, it was fun. Do you think—Could I possibly come with? I'd like to see it happen, however it goes."

"I'm sorry," I said. "We couldn't be responsible for a civilian, too. I think it's going to be a rough one."

"I understand," he replied. "I'd guessed you'd say that, but I had to ask."

I left him there after a time, watching the sky. The moon was still hidden.

And so. . . .

We left before midnight, of course, Jack and I, he in a warm coat and carrying a satchel containing the equipment. Under his other arm, he bore a few small logs for the fire. We left without bothering to lock the door.

The sky was beginning to clear overhead, though the moon was still masked. There was sufficient light just from its glow-through, however, to show our way clearly. There was a chill, damp breeze at our backs.

Soon, Dog's Nest was before us, and Jack decided we should circle it and mount its eastern slope.

We did that, and as we came in sight of the top a small glow was already apparent off in the circle toward the stone with the inscription. Moving nearer, we saw that Vicar Roberts and Morris and MacCab were tending a small fire they had obviously just gotten going, nursing it to achieve greater compass. The vicar's ear was unbandaged now, and light showed through two high perforations in it. The heap of kindling was much larger than when Graymalk and I had been by earlier.

The banefire is a necessary part of our business. It goes all the way back into the misty vastness of our practices. Both sides require it, so in this sense it is a neutral instrument. After midnight, it comes to burn in more than one world, and we may add to it those things which enhance our personal strengths and serve our ends. It attracts otherworldly beings sympathetic to both sides, as well as neutral spirits who may be swayed by the course of the action. Voices and sights may pass through it, and it serves as a secondary, supportive point of manifestation to whatever the opening or closing object may be. Customarily, we all bring something to feed it, and it interacts with all of us throughout the ritual. I had urinated on one of our sticks, for example, several days earlier. There are times when players have been attacked by its flames; and I can recall an instance when one was defended by a sudden wall of fire it issued. It is also good for disposing of evidence. It comes in handy on particularly cold nights, too.

"Good evening," Jack said as we approached, and

he added his contribution to the woodpile.

"Good evening, Jack," the vicar said, and Morris and MacCab nodded.

Lynette lay on her back upon the altar, head turned in our direction, eyes closed, breathing slow. Well drugged, of course. She had on a long white garment, and her dark hair hung loose. I looked away. Obviously, the protest had been overridden. I sniffed the air. No sign of Jill or Graymalk yet.

The fire bloomed more brightly. Jack set his bag down and moved to help with it. I decided on a quick patrol of the area, and I made a big circuit. There was nothing unusual to be found. I went and stared at the huge stone. Just then the edge of the moon appeared from behind the clouds. Its light fell upon it. The markings had become visible again—dark, upon the illuminated surface. I went and sat by Jack's satchel.

The vicar had on a dark cloak which made a swishing sound as he moved. It did not conceal the fact that he was a short, slightly fat man, and it neither added to nor detracted from his appearance of menace. That was all in his face, with its intense expression of controlled mania. The moon was doubled in his glasses.

Under their joint ministrations the banefire grew to a respectable size. The vicar was the first to toss something into it, a small parcel which crackled and flared bluely. I took a sniff. It involved herbs I'd encountered before. Morris added two parcels, which I could tell involved bones. Jack added a very small one which produced a green flash. I tossed in one of my own, along with the pissed-on stick. The moon slid completely free of the clouds.

The vicar went and stared at the inscription, not even glancing at his stepdaughter. Then he backed away, turned to his left, took several paces, halted, turned back toward the stone. He adjusted his position slightly, then scuffed at the ground with his bootheel.

"I will position myself here," he stated, glancing at Jack.

"I have no objection," Jack said. "Your associates will be to your right, I presume?"

"That was what I had in mind. Morris here, MacCab to his right, then Jill," he said, gesturing.

Jack nodded, just as a dark shape swept past the face of the moon. Moments later, Nightwind dropped out of the sky, coming to rest atop the woodpile.

"Hello, Snuff," he observed. "Care to switch?"

"No, thanks. Yourself?"

He did one of those unusual rotations of his head.

"I think not, especially when we outnumber you in all respects."

Shortly, Tekela swept in with a *caw*, landing upon the vicar's left shoulder.

"Greetings, Nightwind," she said.

"A good Game to you, sister."

She looked at me and looked away. She said nothing. Neither did I.

Everyone added more kindling and more ingredients to the fire. Finally, a pair of fairly large logs were set upon it. Many-colored flames played about them, and soon the logs darkened and the fires danced upon their surfaces. A mixture of odors reached me as powders, bones, herbs, fleshy samples of anatomy—both human and other—were added. A few vials of liquid were also dumped upon it, to smolder and produce heavy, crawling ropes of smoke, to flare brightly, briefly. Within the crackling, I seemed to hear a subliminal whispering begin.

I heard Jill's footsteps mounting the northern slope long before she appeared. When she did she was hard to distinguish against the night for several moments, as she had on a hooded black cloak over a long black dress. She looked taller, more slim; and she carried Graymalk, though she set her down immediately when she achieved the level area.

"Good evening," she said, in general. All four men responded.

"Hi, Snuff," Graymalk said, coming up beside me. "It's a good fire already."

"Yes."

"As you can see. . . ."

"You were overridden."

"Did you find Larry?"

"No."

"Oh my."

"There is a backup plan," I said, and Nightwind came by just then, to greet Graymalk.

I felt a strong desire to howl at the moon. It was such a howlable moon. But I restrained myself.

The smell of incense reached me. Jill had just begun casting parcels into the banefire. The moon moved nearer to midheaven.

"How will we know when it is time to begin?" Graymalk asked me.

"When we can talk with the people."

"Of course."

"How's your back?"

"It's all right now. You look fit."

"I'm fine."

We watched the fire for a time. Another log was added, and more packets. The smells became a sweetly seductive bouquet. The flames leaped higher now, changing colors regularly, flickering in the wind. Sharp, tinkling musical sounds came sporadically from their midst, and the sounds of voices rose into and out of audibility. Looking away from it, my gaze was attracted by a new light source. The inscription was beginning to glow. Overhead, the moon had reached midheaven.

"Jack, can you hear me?" I called.

"Loud and clear, Snuff. Well-met by moonlight. What's on your mind?"

"Just checking the time," I said.

Suddenly Nightwind was talking to Morris and MacCab, Tekela to the vicar.

"I guess it's time," Graymalk said, "to take our places."

"It is," I replied.

She went off to collect Jill, who was tossing a final packet into the fire. The air was distorted above its colored flames now, as if it were burning in more than one place simultaneously, and in the shimmering area just about it one could catch glimpses of some of those other places. From somewhere to the north, I heard the howl of a wolf.

The vicar went and stood at the spot he had indicated. Morris and MacCab moved to take up their positions to his right; Nightwind stood atop a rock between them. Then Jill moved to stand beside MacCab, Graymalk next to her but three cat-paces forward. I went and stood near her, Jack to my right. The line was bowed, out away from the big stone, with Jack and the vicar across from each other. Lynette dozed on the altar about ten feet in front of me.

From somewhere within his cloak, the vicar removed the pentacle bowl, which he placed on the ground before him. Then he withdrew the Alhazred Icon, which he propped against a rock to his left, facing the glowing stone. Nightwind moved to a new position, back behind the pentacle. The openers always begin things, as the closers' work is purely reactive.

Jack's satchel, to his right, was already open, from the removal of various ingredients for the banefire, but he leaned and spread its mouth fully, for easy access.

MacCab knelt and spread a piece of white cloth upon the ground before him. As it was windy, he weighted its corners with small stones. Then, from an ornate sheath which hung from his belt beneath his jacket, he drew a long, thin blade which looked to me like a sacrificial knife, and he placed this upon the cloth, point toward the altar.

Then the moon went out. We all looked upward as a dark shape covered it, descending, rushing toward us. Morris shrieked shrilly as it fell, changing shape as if dark veils swam about it. And then the moon shone again, and the piece of midnight sky which had fallen came to earth beside Jack, and I saw that vision-twisting transformation of which Graymalk had spoken—here, there, a twist, a swirl, a dark bending— and the Count stood at Jack's side, smiling a totally evil smile. He laid his left hand—the dark ring visible upon it—upon Jack's right shoulder.

"I stand with him," he said, "to close you out."

Vicar Roberts stared at him and licked his lips.

"I would think one of your sort more inclined to our view in this matter," the vicar stated.

"I like the world just the way it is," said the Count. "Pray, let us begin."

The vicar nodded.

"We shall," he said, "to its proper conclusion, with the Gate thrown wide."

The Count tossed a twig and a small parcel into the flames. The fire moved in its colorful dance, crackling and chiming, burning a hole in the night, through which the voices—now chanting—emerged. Shadows constantly moved past us, over the altar, and across the face of the stone. I heard the howl again, much nearer.

I looked at the vicar and saw him flinch. But he straightened and performed an opening gesture. He spoke a word of power, deeply, slowly. It hung in the air and resonated afterwards.

The inscription on the stone began to glow a little more brightly, and now—very faintly—I could discern the formation of the door-like rectangle come to frame it, that configuration which earlier had sucked Graymalk and me through to our Dreamworld adventure.

The vicar repeated the word and the rectangle came clear.

Within the chanting, I could now hear faintly "Iä! Shub-Niggurath!" being repeated, as if in response. Ahead of me, Graymalk had risen to her feet and was standing very stiffly.

The vicar turned then, rather than proceeding to the next phase, and moved slowly to the cloth on which the sacrificial blade rested. To his rear, I noted that the Alhazred Icon had also begun to glow. He knelt and raised the blade with both hands, bringing it to his lips and kissing it. Then he rose and turned toward the altar, Tekela still upon his shoulder.

And there came a movement from my right, beyond Jack and the Count. Another dark shape was moving to join us.

The vicar had taken but a single step ahead when a great, gray wolf moved into the firelight and rushed past him toward the altar. Larry Talbot had arrived, apparently in reasonable control of his faculties.

He seized hold of the girl's left shoulder with his teeth and dragged her down from the altar. With that rapid backing motion I had seen him employ before, he dragged her quickly before us toward the north, whence he had come, to my right.

The report of a gunshot filled the air and Larry staggered, a dark blot appearing and spreading high upon his left shoulder. The vicar held a smoking revolver, pointed in his direction. Larry continued moving almost immediately, however, and the vicar fired again.

This time there was blood on the top of Larry's head, and he uttered a moaning sound as his jaws fell open and Lynette dropped to the ground. Larry slumped forward then, and the shiftings of firelight and shadow swam over him. The chanting continued— "Iä! Shub-Niggurath!"—against the strange music. The vicar pulled the trigger again. There followed a clicking sound from the pistol, but no discharge. Immediately, he drew it near and worked the hammer. Suddenly, as he released it, there was a sharp report